LIFE LESSONS FROM

ANDY WINK

Steve Paulding

Illustrated by
Ben Spurgin

Design by
Concepts Unlimited
www.ConceptsUnlimitedInc.com

Published by

Slow on the Draw
PRODUCTIONS
LifeLessonsFromAndyWink.com

12826 Ironside Way, #304
Parker, CO 80134
www.LifeLessonsFromAndyWink.com

ISBN: 978-0-615-48469-3   (pbk)

11   12   13   14   15   0 9 8 7 6 5 4 3 2 1

Printed in the USA

Special Thanks

For Mom and Dad for their continued
love and support.

For Libby, Kelly, and Bruce,
three educators who inspire
their students every day.

For Dian, the Grahams, and Preston,
my dearest friends.
I am truly blessed!

A special thanks to my uncle Tommy
for the use of his poem in Chapter 2.

Table of Contents

Introduction

My name is Andy Wink. I'm 12 years old and I'm a 6th grade student at Pine Lane Elementary. I live in Parker, Colorado with my parents, my brother and sister, my dog, and a cat.

Some people say that I'm mature for my age, and they're right. I'm not your average 6th grade student. I see things differently than other 6th graders do as you'll see when you read my book. My philosophy is we're all put on this earth for a reason. I figure the reason that I was put on this earth is simple, to help people out, which is why I wrote *Life Lessons from Andy Wink*.

You see, if you look closely, everyday has a lesson in it, for me and everyone I know. Every day we go through life facing challenges, am I right? Some of the challenges are fun, some of them not so fun, but that doesn't matter. At the end of every challenge, there's always a life lesson. We learn from that lesson and then we move on. We take the life lesson, and what we've learned from it and become better people.

Stinky Steve

1.
The recess football game was approaching its heated climax, and I, Andy Wink, had control of the ball!

"Pass the ball!" Harry Baxter shouted.

My eyes scanned the playing field darting from one teammate to another. The only kid open was Steve Smiley.

"Pass the ball," Harry shouted again. "The recess bell's going to ring!"

I drew back my arm and passed the ball to Steve. The ball sailed through the air, a perfect spiral. Steve reached out, caught the ball, and ran with all of his speed to the end zone. Touchdown! Just as the bell rang.

We lined up, the smell of victory radiating from our bodies. But I also smelled a different smell radiating from Steve Smiley. I couldn't figure out what the smell was! It smelled like my older brother Lance after one of his football games. My brother smelled bad after those games! My sister always told him how bad he smelled and my mom would make him take a shower before she hugged him. I wondered if Steve was like my brother.

I went upstairs and put my football in my backpack. My backpack was next to Steve's. I could still smell the smell! What was it? I walked into my classroom.

"Clear off your desks," Mrs. Higgins said. "There should be

3

nothing on your desks but a pencil."

The class groaned. It was time for our math test. As Mrs. Higgins passed out our test, the smell hit me again! I looked around to find the source of that smell. Steve Smiley looked at me and grinned. I couldn't believe it! The smell was coming from Steve! Steve was stinky! He had this gross, sour, stinky smell around him! Steve kept smiling. He was obviously still happy from our victory.

That night I took a shower and went to bed. As I stared at the ceiling, I thought about my day. A small drop of water ran down my cheek from my wet hair. I hoped that Steve Smiley had taken a shower tonight too.

The next day outside of school, there was a crowd of kids standing around Steve Smiley. They were calling him names.

"Stinky Steve, Stinky Steve, that smell we smell is Stinky Steve!"

The morning bell rang. The kids walked away as I approached Steve.

"Hi Steve," I said.

"Hi Andy," Steve mumbled softly.

Steve had a sad look on his face. I took a deep breath and smiled awkwardly at Steve. Phew! The other kids were right. Steve was stinky!

I felt sorry for Steve. Steve was a great guy! He told funny stories, which made everyone laugh. He played with everyone at recess, and Steve was the best at every sport. But today Steve smelled! I liked Steve and considered him to be one of my best friends, but no one wants to be around someone who smells. I decided I would find a way to help Steve. I wasn't sure how to help him but I knew who to ask. One of the wisest men I know, my dad.

The next morning I decided to talk with my dad about Steve. My dad always has a smart, sensible answer for everything. I looked for my dad and found him in the bathroom getting ready for his day.

"Dad," I said knocking on the bathroom door, "are you decent?"

I laughed at myself, having heard someone say this on TV.

"What is it Andy?" my dad replied.

"I've got a problem at school," I answered.

"Come on in." I walked into the bathroom. "What kind of problem?" my dad asked.

I loved the way my dad smelled in the morning. He was standing in front of the mirror shaving with a towel wrapped around his waist. He took his razor and ran it up one side of his face and then the other.

"It's about Steve Smiley."

"What about Steve?" my dad asked, shaving under his nose.

"Well, I..." I hesitated.

"Is Steve okay?" my dad asked, a look of concern coming over his face.

"Steve stinks!" I quickly exclaimed.

My dad chuckled as he wiped the remaining shaving cream off his face with a towel. He carefully put on some aftershave and reached for his deodorant stick. These were the smells I loved about my dad.

"Does he smell all the time, or just some times?" my dad asked.

"All of the time."

"Well you know Andy," Dad chuckled again, "when little boys become big boys they start to smell like young men."

"What do you mean?" I asked.

"Well, when boys grow older, their bodies change, and with that change come different odors, different sweat, and different hygiene needs. You remember that talk we had, don't you?"

"Yeah," I answered.

"Do you think Steve Smiley has had that talk with his dad?"

"Steve doesn't have a dad," I answered sadly.

Dad thought for a moment. I knew this was it, Dad's problem solving at its best. After a few more seconds, Dad had come up with a solution.

"Why don't you ask Steve over? You know, for a sleepover?"

I think I knew my dad's plan.

It was Friday night. Steve and I ordered pizza for dinner, watched scary movies, and then headed for bed.

The next morning I woke up and took a shower. After a few minutes I got out of the shower and wrapped a towel around my waist the way my dad had done. I put some shaving cream on my face and carefully began to shave.

"Hey," Steve asked, "what are you doing?"

"I'm shaving," I answered.

"You're not old enough to shave!" exclaimed Steve.

"Sure I am. I've got a couple of hairs! Of course my mom teases me and calls it peach fuzz."

Steve laughed. I shaved as carefully as I could without cutting myself as Steve watched. When I finished, I wiped off the remaining shaving cream with a towel, and splashed some aftershave on my face. Trying not to scream from the sting of the aftershave like the kid from *Home Alone*, I reached for a deodorant stick.

"Why are you putting on deodorant?" Steve asked.

"Because I sweat," I answered, "and when I sweat, I stink."

I reached into a cabinet and pulled out a new deodorant stick.

"Here Steve, this is for you."

"What's this?" Steve asked, "Are you saying that I'm Stinky Steve?"

Once again Steve looked hurt.

"No," I answered, "I'm saying that your body is changing just like mine. My dad says we're becoming young men, and unless you want to be stinky, we need to use things like this. Besides, he says smelling great is a way to get girls to notice us."

This brought a smile to Steve's face. Steve showered and shaved, and I laughed when his eyes watered as he put cologne on his face.

As the years passed, Steve became quarterback of our high school football team. He dated the most beautiful girls in our school, and he was crowned Homecoming King!

After I went away to college, I lost touch with Steve, but I'll lay you odds, the day after our sleepover, Steve never had a Stinky Steve problem again!

GOD HAS PROMISED ME HIS HEAVEN,
HIS HOME WAY UP ABOVE,
WHERE THERE WILL BE NO PAIN
OR HATRED,
ONLY HIS ETERNAL LOVE.
THERE WON'T BE ANY DARKNESS,
FOR HIS LOVE IT SHINES SO BRIGHT,
AND ANYWHERE THAT I MAY GO, I'LL BE
WALKING IN HIS LIGHT.

The Poem

2. I was walking down the school hallway one morning when I saw a piece of paper lying on the floor. It was neatly folded and, well, you know me being "green" and everything, I stopped to pick up the paper and headed toward the nearest recycling box to throw it away.

Before I reached the box I noticed that the paper wasn't just a piece of paper, but a poem that someone had written. I carefully unfolded the piece of paper and began to read...

When He comes to take me home, I hope my friends don't cry.
For in my heart, I've always known that a Christian never dies.
God has promised me His heaven, His home way up above,
where there will be no pain or hatred, only His eternal love.
There won't be any darkness, for His love it shines so bright,
and anywhere that I may go, I'll be walking in His light.
Don't think that I have left you, I'll be with you every day,
I'll be there when you slip and fall,
I'll hear you when you pray.
Then someday, we will meet again, to never ever part,
so death my friends is not the end, but rather a brand new start.
So when at last He takes me home, how happy I will be, and
as you gather one and all, oh please don't cry for me.

I was blown away by the beauty of the poem. I looked up and down the hallway for its author but the hallway was empty. I carefully tucked the poem into my back pocket, thinking to myself that I had to find the person who wrote it, and I, Andy Wink, was going to return it to its rightful owner!

After dinner, I was in the living room sitting in our over-sized comfy sofa when my dad asked, "What ya got there, Andy?"

"I found this poem on the floor in the hallway at school. I was just reading it again."

"Is it any good?" my dad asked.

"Yeah," I answered, "it's good."

My dad took the poem from my hands and read it silently. Every few seconds he would let out a "hmmm," or "uh huh."

He handed it back to me asking, "Who wrote this? It's very well written."

"I don't know," I answered, "but I'd like to find out. I'd like to talk with them about why they wrote this poem, and ask them if I could read some of their other writing."

Later that night I lay in my bed and thought about the day. I kept coming back to the poem. I kept wondering to myself, "Who wrote it?" The next day I started out on my journey to find the author.

Every school has many different kinds of kids. By different I mean normal kids, greasers, heavy metal followers. I decided to start with the normal kid.

Ben Randall was about as "normal" as you could get. He

never did anything that any teacher or grown up would ever have to worry about. Ben's hair was short and neat, and he had this preppie style of dress: jeans, polo shirt, and tennis shoes. I approached Ben at morning recess as he was shooting baskets.

"Hi Ben."

"Hi Andy, want to shoot some hoops?" he asked.

"Sure," I answered, never being one to turn down any kind of sport.

After a couple of games of one-on-one, I decided to ask Ben about the poem.

"Hey Ben?"

"Yeah," he answered, sweat running down his face.

"I found this poem in the hallway and I was wondering if you knew who wrote it? Or maybe you wrote it?"

"What's it about?" Ben asked.

"It's about what happens after we die," I answered.

"That's way too deep for me!" Ben answered sarcastically.

I knew right away that I hadn't found the author.

"I can't write, Andy," Ben said wiping his face with his shirt, "as a matter of fact I hate to write! It's hard for me to put my thoughts together and the teachers are always talking about sequencing. I don't get sequencing!"

"Sequencing's easy! It's the order of the story, you know, the beginning, middle, and end?"

"Give me a video game any day," Ben replied, "that's what I'm good at."

Ben was also good at ending his sentence with a preposition!

Ben gave me a high five and headed into the school as the recess bell rang.

I decided to approach Parker Cushing. Parker Cushing was a "greaser." He always wore his hair in a duck tail, and he wore jeans that were folded over at the bottom. He worshipped Elvis Presley, and Parker was always carrying around his guitar. The teachers hated Parker's guitar and always made him "check it" at the classroom door. I approached Parker at lunch.

"Hi Parker!"

Parker spun around. He was holding his guitar and he gyrated his hips as he asked, "Hey Wink, what's shaking?"

"Ah... nothing."

Parker took a bite out of his Choice B grilled cheese sandwich.

"I can't believe how soggy these sandwiches are! I mean how can they mess up a grilled cheese sandwich?"

"They microwave them in plastic bags," I answered, "so the moisture on the inside of the bag makes the sandwich soggy."

"Wellllllll Buuuuuuuudy," he answered in a really bad Elvis Presley imitation, "that explains a lot!"

Parker gyrated and swayed his hips a little and waited for me to make my next comment.

"Listen, Parker. I found this poem in the hallway, and I thought maybe you might know who wrote it, or maybe you wrote it, but I doubt it."

"You're right Wink! I don't write poetry, I'm true to my music!"

"So you have no idea who might have lost this poem?"

I took the poem out of my back pocket and Parker took it out of my hand.

"What's it about?" Parker asked. "Can I put the words to music?"

"Not your kind of music," I answered under my breath.

Parker put the poem on the table and began to strum some very long chords as he began to sing.

"When he comes to take me home (loud chord) I hope my friends don't cry (loud chord.)"

All of a sudden Parker exploded into a loud rock and roll hip gyrating song.

"For in my heart I've always known that a Christian never dies!"

Parker suddenly stopped playing.

"Sorry Buddy, I didn't write this."

"I didn't think so," I answered.

"It ain't rock and roll."

"No, it isn't," I agreed.

Parker folded the poem and handed it back to me.

"Thanks for trying Parker," I said, as I put the poem back into my back pocket and walked away.

Doug Mickelsen's a Heavy Metal follower. He's nice, but he's really into Heavy Metal. He has really blonde hair and he idolizes

David Lee Roth and Bon Jovi. He always wears a black Van Halen or Metalica t-shirt. Doug is opposed to "poseur-rock," and "hair band," and he really makes a point of not having anything to do with that kind of music. Doug once beat up a kid on the playground for calling him an Emo, and Doug is very anti-authority!

"Mr. Mickelsen! If you don't quiet down, I'm going to ask you to leave this library!"

"This library," Doug said as he looked at me, "like we're in any other library!"

Ms. Nutt the librarian threw Doug the "quiet down look."

Sadly, Doug Mickelsen and I were social studies partners, which meant that I might as well be working by myself. We were supposed to be working on a South American project. Our country was Argentina. We were supposed to come up with a tri-fold brochure that would make the class want to come and visit our country. The project was a disaster from the start! Not only was I working with Doug Mickelsen, but what did Argentina have to offer? Coffee? The Drug Cartel? Argentina might be nice to the people who live there, but it isn't a very valuable country on a RISK board!

I wanted to ask Doug about the poem, but I was pretty sure he hadn't written it, so I didn't bother.

As we continued to sit in the library staring at each other, not working on our project, Doug Mickelsen suddenly started to play the imaginary air guitar, pretending to be Tommy Lee.

Ms. Nutt got up from her chair and took him to the office. That was the end of our project and the end of Argentina! I was put in a group with Jonathan Cohen and Ryan Denton. Their country was Brazil. Also not worth much on a RISK board, but at least you could cross into Africa.

Mackenzie Cassidy's a tomboy. She reminds me of Jodie Foster in every one of her movies. Blonde, butch, and tough! At recess, Mackenzie pitches the meanest, fastest baseball I've ever seen, and no one wants to play catcher opposite her pitch! I loved baseball and I didn't mind catching when Mackenzie pitched, even though my hand stung for hours afterward.

That afternoon at recess, Jeff Kinney was the next one up to bat. He was kind of a wimpy kid so I knew he wouldn't hit it very far. Mackenzie Cassidy gave me a look.

"Oh crap," I thought, "she wants a signal for what kind of ball to pitch. What was the signal for slow ball?" I wondered.

I put down two fingers, maybe three, I didn't remember. Mackenzie got ready to throw the ball. The ball shot like a laser coming straight for me. Jeff Kinney closed his eyes and swung the bat. He tipped the ball, not slowing it down at all. I put my glove in front of my face, my life flashing before my eyes. I caught the ball, Jeff Kinney was out, but the force of the pitch caused me to stumble back and hit my head on the fence behind me. I landed flat on my back, out like a light.

I remember waking up, feeling dizzy and just staring up at the sky. I saw a bird fly in front of a cloud. Mackenzie Cassidy leaned over me blocking my view of the sky, the birds, and the clouds.

"Did you write a poem about what happens after you die?" I asked her deliriously.

"No. I'm taking you to the nurse," she answered.

After checking me out for what I'm sure was a concussion, the nurse told me I should lie down but not go to sleep. That didn't make sense to me. The only time I laid down was to go to sleep.

There were only two of us in the health room, me and Jacob Boyd.

Jacob Boyd is one of the nicest people at our school! I guess you could say he was a jock because he was good at every sport, but he was also good at music and art. Everybody at our school loves Jacob Boyd! He always fits in with every group and clique. It didn't matter if you were normal, a greaser, a heavy metal follower, a tomboy, or a jock, everyone accepted Jacob into their group. Maybe it's because he always has a positive, can do, attitude about everything! He's supportive to everyone and it doesn't matter who you are. Jacob is a leader, and it seems like he has everything, but he doesn't.

When Jacob was a little boy, his father walked out on him and his mother. No one knows why. Maybe it was because his father couldn't handle the responsibilities of raising a family, maybe it was because he couldn't provide for his family; who knows? Sometimes there aren't answers for things that happen to people in life, and that's one of the biggest life lessons.

"What are you in for?" I joked, having seen one too many prison movies.

"I have a fever and I'm light headed," Jacob answered, as he tried to sit up. "I can't be sick. I need to help my mom after school."

I knew that Jacob did odd jobs after school to help make ends meet.

"How are you doing Jake?" the nurse asked, as she walked into the Health room and felt Jacob's forehead.

"I'm so tired," he answered, lying back down.

"Your mother will be here in a little while," she said, as she put a blanket over him and put her hand on his cheek. "If you need anything, I'm right outside the door."

Jacob Boyd was also the best looking guy at our school. His looks attracted every girl at our school and that obviously included the school nurse!

"Uh, I'm fine too," I said raising my hand and waving at the nurse.

"I'm sure you are Andy," the nurse said, as she patted my head and left the room.

Jacob has these piercing blue eyes, and he has short spiky blonde hair. He usually wore the same designer jeans, and he has several athletic fit shirts. He always wears a necklace that I admired. It hung from a piece of very thin leather and it was rectangular and silver. There was no doubt about it, Jacob Boyd was a one in a million kid, which is probably another reason that everyone accepted him into their lives.

I remembered back to when we were both in Cub Scouts and we had a sleep over at the Dinosaur Museum. Everyone's father was there except for Jacob's, so my dad and I invited him over to stay with us. We told ghost stories, ate snacks, laughed, and just forgot about everything, every problem we ever had.

That night, before we went to sleep underneath the T-Rex, Jacob thanked me for letting him be a part of my family. He told me when he grew up, he was going to be the best dad ever and do things with his kids all of the time, the way my dad did things with his kids.

I stood up and looked at myself in the Health Room mirror. My hair was a mess! I pulled my comb out of my back pocket, and the poem came out with it, and fell to the floor.

"Hey, where did you find that?" Jacob asked. "That's my poem."

"I found it on the floor in the hallway," I answered, "I was trying to figure out who wrote it."

"You read it?" Jacob asked.

"Yeah, it's very good. I didn't know you could write like this."

"I wrote it in memory of my grandmother. She died a few weeks ago."

"I'm sorry Jake."

"I like to write. When I write I can forget about everything. Sometimes my writing takes me to places that I've never been. It introduces me to people and things I've never known. But most of all my writing gives me my voice, my voice that other people have never heard before."

"Your Mother's here," the nurse said as she popped her head into the room.

"Thanks," Jacob answered as he slowly got up and headed toward the door.

"Jake, have you written anything else?" I asked.

"Yeah, sure, lots of things."

"Do you think we could get together and I could read them sometime?"

"Sure, but not today," he said with a soft laugh. "Hope you're feeling better Andy."

"You too Jake," I answered.

Jake slowly walked out of the Health Room.

I laid down and stared at the ceiling. It was a funny thing about Jacob Boyd and the poem. I guess I had learned not to pass judgment on anyone until I really got to know them. The poem could have been written by anyone, but it was written by the person I would have least expected.

Jacob and I did get together and I read some more of his writing. He'd written a couple of short stories, some more poetry, and was beginning a book on how we should take care of our planet, which made him a bigger hero to me than he'd ever been before.

The School Play

3. **It was time for the school play, and I, Andy Wink was going to try out for a part!**

Our school was putting on the play *The Adventures of Tom Sawyer* by Mark Twain.

The Adventures of Tom Sawyer is the story of a fourteen-year-old boy who grows up in St. Petersburg, Missouri on the banks of the Mississippi River. Tom has a best friend named Huckleberry Finn. The two of them witness a murder, but best of all, Tom Sawyer falls in love with a girl named Becky Thatcher and he gets to kiss her!

The part of Becky Thatcher would almost certainly be played by Mary Ann Miller. Mary Ann Miller is the cutest girl in school! She has long yellow hair which she always wears in braids and she has the cutest little freckles on her cheeks and nose. If Mary Ann Miller is cast as Becky Thatcher, I have to play Tom Sawyer! There is only one problem... Vander Erickson!

Vander Erickson is Mr. Shakespeare himself! He always gets cast in the lead part in every school play! By lead part I mean the main part! In this case, the part of Tom Sawyer! The part of the boy who gets to kiss the girl!

In case you haven't noticed, I'm a little jealous of Vander Erickson. Vander Erickson comes from a family of actors. His mom and dad do a lot of community theatre, his grandpa's on a TV soap opera, and his little sister competes in all of those Little Miss Sunshine beauty pageants... if you can call that acting!

Vander Erickson's even been in a TV commercial! It was for Chomps Dog Food. Vander even had a line! He got to say, "Here boy!" as a hungry golden retriever ran to him for his supper.

Vander Erickson also takes acting and dancing lessons. He's what people in the acting business call a triple threat: He can act; he can sing; he can dance. I can't do any of the three, except maybe act... maybe.

"What are you doing?" asked my dad as he walked into the study.

Red in the face I answered, "I'm memorizing my monologue so that I can try out for the school play."

"The school play?" my dad asked.

"Yeah Dad, the school play. You have to memorize a one-minute monologue to try out. They're doing *The Adventures of Tom Sawyer* and I really want to play Tom!"

"Wow Andy! This is a side of you I've never seen before! You're usually involved in sports: golf, football, or baseball. What made you want to audition for the school play?"

Suddenly there was a long pause that felt like it lasted forever! Did I tell my dad the truth? That I really wanted to kiss Mary Ann Miller, or did I act like trying out for the school play was no big deal?

"I want to broaden my horizons!"

There it was, my big grown-up sentence for the day (you know I always try to say at least one.) Talk like a grown-up. Horizons means do or learn about other things that you normally wouldn't do.

"Broaden your horizons?" my dad asked skeptically. "Well, okay, let's hear it!"

"Hear it?" I asked nervously.

"Your monologue! Run it by me!"

Suddenly I was scared! I felt like Ben Kramer, the biggest bully at school, had punched me in the stomach, twisted his arm as far as he could, pulled out all of my guts, and left them to sizzle on the hot sidewalk! I wanted to perform my monologue for my dad, but suddenly I had butterflies in my stomach! Would I feel this scared when I tried out for the play?

"Andy?" my dad snapped me out of my daze, "I'm ready."

"What? Yeah..." I answered, "I've been working really hard so go easy on me, with any criticism I mean."

"Just do the best you can Andy," my dad said, as he made himself comfortable in his easy chair.

I lowered my head and closed my eyes. I cleared my mind of any thoughts. I raised my head and said, "How do you do? My name's Andy Wink and I will be performing a monologue from Henry V by William Shakespeare." (I wanted the part of Tom badly!)

A look of surprise came over my dad's face.

"That's the way we're supposed to do it," I said, "Mr. Severns, our drama teacher, said we should introduce ourselves and name the play the monologue's from."

"Go on Andy," my dad encouraged.

I imagined myself in an amazing castle. Seated on a throne in front of me was a beautiful queen dressed in a white dress. Suddenly I became the character I was trying out as. I began...

"No Kate? I will tell you then in French, which I'm sure I will hang upon my tongue like a new married wife about her husband's neck, hardly to be shook off. *Je quarde sur le possession de France, et quand vous avez le possession de moi,* let me see, what then?"

My dad started to laugh. He wasn't laughing at me, he was laughing with me as I butchered the French language like a garbage disposal grinds up left-over food.

"Oh Saint Denis be my speed!" I laughed, "*Done votre est France et vous etes mienne.* It is easy for me Kate, to conquer the kingdom as to speak so much more French, I shall never move thee in French, unless it be to laugh at me."

When I finished, a hush fell over the study followed by a long pause. Had my monologue been okay? Was my dad impressed, or was he trying to figure out something nice to say. I felt a calm come over me. I knew deep down inside that I had done well... really well!

My dad started to clap.

"Andy," my dad exclaimed, "that's about the best

monologue I've ever heard! And Shakespeare? What made you choose Shakespeare?"

"I saw Henry V last month on Starz," I answered, "I got the monologue online. I thought it would impress Mr. Severns."

"Well you certainly impressed me Andy! You certainly impressed me! I am so proud of you!"

I knew my dad was telling the truth. He wasn't trying to make me feel good because I was his son. I had blown my dad away with my monologue and I could blow Vander Erickson away too!

The Peanuts character Charlie Brown used to say that lunchtime was among the worst times of the day. He was right.

I was sitting in the lunch room eating my Choice A, soggy pizza, when I felt someone sit in the seat next to me. It was Vander Erickson. I would have recognized that imposter designer cologne anywhere!

"How're you doing Wink?" he asked in a smarmy tone.

I don't like it when people call me by my last name, and I especially don't like it when Vander Erickson calls me by my last name! One time I saw him in the hall and he yelled, "How's it going Wink a blink?" and I wanted to knocked his lights out! It isn't that I don't like my last name, because I do, and it would be different if I was an adult. If I was an adult, I'd be known as Mr. Wink, or if I was a professional baseball player the announcer would say, "Now coming to the plate in the bottom of the ninth, Andy Wink!" that would be okay too. It's just at my age, I prefer to be called Andy.

"What are you up to?" Vander asked, trying to get my attention again.

"Just eating my soggy pizza."

"I don't have that problem Wink!"

"Argh!" I screamed in my mind!

"My mom sends a nutritious lunch to school with me every day," he continued.

Vander opened his lunch box and began to take out his lunch as he spoke.

"Ham and cheese sandwich, bag of chips, a thermos full of hot soup, fruit that's in season, and a bottle of pomegranate juice to wash it all down with!"

I didn't understand what was happening. Vander Erickson never sat by me at lunch! He always sat, well, by himself. Vander finished unpacking his lunch box as he continued to talk.

"So Wink?"

"Argh!"

"I see you signed up to audition for the school play."

"Yeah..." my voice quivered, "I'd like to try out. I think it would be fun."

"Try outs are for cheerleaders Wink! People audition for the school play!"

There was an awkward pause as Vander began to eat his lunch and talk with his mouth full.

"I guess you know that I've had the lead in every school play since I started going to this school. Did you see any of my performances?"

"I must have been busy."

"Too bad, because I was very good! Did you happen to catch my Chomps Dog Food commercial?" he pushed on.

"No, I guess I missed that too," I answered.

I knew right away where this conversation was going. Vander Erickson was trying to bully me so that I wouldn't audition for the school play.

"What I'm getting at Wink is that you probably shouldn't waste your time auditioning. Especially for the lead, I'm too much competition! No one at this school can beat me when it comes to acting!"

I could feel myself getting mad. If I'd been a thermometer you could have seen my temperature rising!

"You might think you're the best actor at this school, but that doesn't make it true!"

I couldn't believe what I had just said! I had popped off to one of the most popular and conceited boys in school.

"What's that Wink?" Vander stared in disbelief.

"You can't play all of the parts!" I said loudly.

I couldn't believe it! I'd done it again! Popped off I mean!

"What?"

Vander was at a complete loss of words.

"What?" he asked again, cocking his head to one side.

I could tell I'd touched a nerve. Vander Erickson was shocked and in a state of disbelief at what I had said, and he was getting angry. He felt threatened because I was auditioning for the school play! Vander quickly started to put his food back into his lunch box.

"You just remember this Wink! Nobody's going to take the lead away from me! Nobody! I'm going to play the part of Tom Sawyer or I don't know what!"

Vander took a small mirror out of his pocket. He checked his teeth for food, put the mirror away, got up, and strutted away.

"Wow!" I thought to myself, "he's really high maintenance!"

There was only one class that stood between me and my audition for the school play and that class was P.E. It was one of my favorite classes! It always helped me to take my mind off my problems, except for today. Vander Erickson was in my P.E. class, and he kept squinting his eyes at me and giving me the evil eye.

We were playing baseball. Our coach would pitch a baseball to us and we would try to hit it. I was a natural. I'd been playing baseball since I was five years old. Vander on the other hand was terrible. Finally something he couldn't do, which made me very happy.

I stepped into the batter's box. I shouldered the bat and the coach pitched the ball to me. I swung and hit the ball into the outfield. I did it again, and again, and again.

Next it was Vander's turn. He stood outside of the batter's box, weakly held up the bat, and tried to swing at the ball. He looked like he was swatting flies. He missed the ball again, and again, and again.

"You need to step into the batter's box," I said.

Another ball whizzed by.

"If I want your help Wink, I'll ask for it!" Vander said angrily.

Another ball whizzed by.

"Andy," the coach yelled, "get in there and help him!"

"Great!" I thought to myself. "Ok Coach!" I answered.

I walked over to Vander.

"So now what Wink?" he asked. "You going to be a teacher now too?"

"You need to step into the batter's box," I instructed.

"What?" Vander asked.

"You need to step into the batter's box, and you need to keep your eyes on the ball."

I showed Vander where to stand.

"Stand here and keep your eyes on the ball."

I stepped away from the batter's box as the Coach threw another ball. Vander swung and missed.

"Crap!" he yelled, "I can't do it!"

"Watch the language," Coach warned, "Andy, tell Erickson about 'the wiggle'!"

"The wiggle?" Vander asked. "What the heck's he talking about Wink?"

"It's how to hit the ball. You need to bend your knees, and you need to wiggle your butt," I explained.

"Come on Wink!" Vander said in disbelief.

"I'm not kidding! Keep your eyes on the ball, bend your knees, and wiggle your butt," I repeated, "let me show you."

I took the bat from Vander, shouldered the bat, bent my knees, and started to wiggle my butt.

"You look stupid!" Vander exclaimed.

Just as Vander said the word stupid, the coach pitched me a ball and with a loud crack, I hit it into the outfield.

"That's amazing," Vander uttered under his breath.

I handed Vander the bat and repeated what I had said.

"Eyes on the ball, bend your knees, and wiggle your butt."

Vander stepped into the batter's box whispering over and over again, "Eyes on the ball, bend my knees, and wiggle my butt. Eyes on the ball, bend my knees, and wiggle my butt."

Vander looked funny. He had the worst wiggle I'd ever seen. He swung his hips from side to side like he was twirling a hula hoop.

"You boys ready?" Coach asked.

"Ready Coach," I answered confidently.

I stepped away from Vander as far as I could. Who knew

where he would hit the ball if he connected? Vander bent his knees and began to wiggle as Coach leaned back and threw the ball toward the batter's box. Vander closed his eyes and swung with all of his might.

I can't remember ever hearing such a loud crack when a bat connected with a baseball. Vander opened his eyes just in time to see the ball sail over the outfield fence. "Homerun!" Coach yelled. I smiled as Vander started to circle the bases. He obviously didn't remember that this wasn't a real game.

"I DID IT, I DID IT," he kept repeating as he rounded the bases, "I DID IT!"

When Vander crossed home plate, he was so excited, he jumped at me and I had no choice but to catch him.

"I did it Wink! I really did it!" He shouted.

I gently set Vander down on the ground.

"Yeah Van, you did great," I said, feeling more comfortable with him. I leaned toward him.

"But I could have done without the jumping into my arms part."

"Sorry about that," Vander said gasping for breath.

"It was the wiggle," I said smiling.

"The wiggle," Vander agreed, as he bent over trying to catch his breath.

"Time to go in!" Coach shouted.

The class picked up the baseball equipment and headed inside. Vander and I walked in together.

"Thanks for your help Andy," he said.

"Andy? Did I hear him right?" I thought to myself.

"Listen," he continued, "I'm sorry about lunch earlier. I really want to play Tom Sawyer, but you're good, you're good at everything you do, and I bet you're a good actor too."

"I don't know if I am or not," I answered, "but I want to try. Who knows what will happen? There are a bunch of kids trying..." I stopped myself, "auditioning, and maybe neither one of us will get to play Tom. But if that happens, that's okay too. There are a lot of other great parts! There's Huckleberry Finn, and Muff Potter, there's Injun Joe, and all of the kids that whitewash the fence, and then there's Cousin Sydney! He's the smartest kid in school, he's snotty..."

I stopped in my tracks. Vander turned toward me.

"Vander," I said, "you'd make a perfect Cousin Sydney! He's the smartest kid in school, he's snotty..."

I realized what I was saying, stopped mid sentence, shut my mouth, and started to walk again. I decided to quit talking while I was ahead.

After auditions Mr. Severns said he would post the cast list the next morning.

I tossed and turned in my bed all night! I thought my audition had gone well but not as good as when I had performed it for my dad. Mr. Severns said that he was impressed that I had "tackled" Shakespeare.

The next morning as I walked into school there was a huge

crowd of kids around the theatre bulletin board. Some were laughing and congratulating each other, some of the girls were crying. I took a deep breath and walked toward the crowd. Vander Erickson was looking at the cast list. He turned and walked past me.

"Congratulations Andy," he said.

My heart started to race. I started to feel short of breath. I'd never experienced the anxiety of looking at a cast list before. I felt like I was going to pass out.

All of a sudden, my brain shifted into high gear! Vander Erickson had congratulated me, so I must have gotten something! I made my way through the crowd of kids and started to read the cast list. My eyes started at the top of the list and made their way down.

Tom Sawyer— Vander Erickson. My heart sank. Vander had gotten the part of Tom.

My eyes started to tear up. "Hold it together Andy," I said to myself. I continued down the cast list. Aunt Polly— Olivia Thomas, Cousin Sydney— Luke Stratman, Cousin Mary— Alison Story, Muff Potter— Conor Stewartson, Becky Thatcher— Mary Ann Miller.

I let out a small sob.

Huckleberry Finn— Andy Wink.

A rush of adrenalin shot through my body! There was my name! I was playing the part of Huckleberry Finn, Tom's best friend! How ironic was it that Vander and I would be playing best friends?

"Congratulations Andy."

I turned to see who was talking to me.

"I'm glad you got the part of Huckleberry Finn."

It was Mary Ann Miller!

"Uh, thanks," I said. I couldn't come up with any intelligent response. I was shell shocked!

"You've never been in a school play before, have you?" she asked.

"No," I said pulling myself together, "this is my first one."

"They're a lot of fun," she laughed. "We get to rehearse together, and when we're not on stage, we do our homework together, we help each other with our lines..."

"Things are looking up," I thought to myself, as she continued to talk. "This was fantastic! I was going to be spending a lot of time with Mary Ann Miller!"

"Andy?" she asked, snapping me out of my thoughts. "I'm glad that you're a part of our show."

Mary Ann Miller leaned over and gave me a quick kiss on the cheek, and then she was gone. As I watched her walk away, I thought I was going to pass out!

Every performance of *The Adventures of Tom Sawyer* sold out and I loved playing the part of Huckleberry Finn! I got to wear overalls, I got to go barefoot, I got to pretend to smoke a corn cob pipe, but best of all, I got to spit out cuss words (my brother Lance was really jealous about that)! Playing the part of Huckleberry Finn was great because I got to do everything I never got to do as Andy Wink.

But most of all, I got to spend a lot of time with Mary Ann Miller, and Mary Ann Miller eventually became Mrs. Mary Ann Wink, but that's another story.

Carved

4. James Gunn's new horror movie *Carved* starts tomorrow at the Cinema Center, and I, Andy Wink, will be one of the first ones in line to see it! (That is if I can talk my mom and dad into letting me go.)

I love horror movies and I love being scared when I go to horror movies! The more murder, mayhem, and blood letting the better! I love it when a truck load of teenagers get lost in the woods and one by one they fall into the hands, or paws, of a psycho path, zombie, or mutant animal!

There they are on the screen, the teenage pillars of our society! The most perfect looking teenagers in the world! Guys and girls with perfect teeth, guys and girls wearing preppie clothes, guys with perfect abs, girls with perfect... well you know where I'm going with that, and they're all getting wiped off the planet one by one because they either have to explore that sound over there, use the bathroom behind that tree, check out the cellar, get into a car that never starts, or split up so that whoever or whatever's stalking them can kill them one by one when they're in smaller groups. And let's face it, if a guy and girl have just finished making out they're always the first ones to die. It's true! If a guy or girl have just finished making out they're always the first ones to die in a horror movie, unless there's a guy of color, or someone in a wheelchair, then they're always the first ones to die!

Okay! I know what you're thinking! Don't get on my case because I said guy of color, or person in a wheelchair! One of my best friends is black, and one of my classmates is in a wheelchair and I always help him when he needs help. Besides, I'm not the one who writes the horror movie rule book!

James Gunn has always been my favorite horror movie director! He directed *Tromeo and Juliet* and *Slither*, he wrote the re-make of *Dawn of the Dead*, and he wrote the screenplay for *Scooby-Doo* and *Scooby Doo 2: Monsters Unleashed*. I didn't see either one of those movies, but I guess everybody has to sell out at least a couple of times in their life to make enough money to do what they love to do, and that's to make horror movies!

Dinner is one of the most sacred times of the day. It's one of the things that holds a family together. At dinner my family talks about our day, we argue, sometimes my siblings and I will give each other the business, or get into each other's business, and dinner is where we announce our plans for the next day or the upcoming weekend.

"Kyle, Jett, Grant, and I would like to go to the movies tomorrow night," I said, staring down at the uneaten peas on my plate.

"That's great," my dad responded, "Your mom and I saw an ad on TV for *I've Got the Ring and You've Got the Finger*, it looked funny didn't it dear?"

"Yes it did," my mom agreed.

I raised my head and looked at my brother who had a wicked grin on his face.

"Who's in that movie?" my dad asked my mom.

"Ashton Kutcher, I think," my mom answered.

"What TV show was he on?" my dad asked.

"I think he was one of those 'Friends'," my mom answered.

I looked at my sister who rolled her head back, and then rolled her eyes back as far as her head would let her.

"Well whoever it is, it sure looks funny! We may have to see that one," my dad stated.

"He doesn't want to see the finger movie," my brother Lance butted in, "he wants to see *Carved!*"

I quickly looked at my brother, giving him a "thanks for stabbing me in the back" look.

"*Carved?*" my dad asked laughing, "what's that one about, a Thanksgiving turkey?"

My dad laughed out loud because he thought what he said was funny, but I could tell my sister had had enough of the dinner table conversation.

"May I be excused, please? I'm not feeling well," she said.

"Isn't it your turn to clear the table?" my mom asked.

"I set the table," she answered.

"I set the table," I corrected her.

"I took out the trash," my sister said looking for excuses.

41

I could tell that my sister wanted to get out of the dinner conversation badly. She probably had to text someone or tweet. My parents knew that if they let her get away from the table, she'd disappear into her bedroom and they wouldn't see her again until dinner sometime next year.

"I took out the trash," my brother said staring my sister down.

"I think you'd better help clear," my mom said, picking up my plate of uneaten peas.

"Why don't we make a family evening out of it?" my dad asked, "Tomorrow night we can all go see *I've Got the Ring and You've Got the Finger!*"

"Dad, I just told you that I want to go to the movie with some friends."

"Yeah, to see *Carved*," my brother pointed out again.

My brother Lance worked at the Cinema Center and he knew everything about every movie so he was quick to give a synopsis.

"It's about a van full of teenagers who get lost on Thanksgiving night in a rainstorm and they get stuck in a farmer's field, and the farmer has a lot of sharp tools that he uses to kill them with," my brother slowed down the end of his sentence to make a point, "one, by, one!"

I couldn't believe what I was hearing. Suddenly my brother had become my enemy!

"And," my brother continued, "it's rated R, for extreme sex

42

and violence!"

"Extreme," I thought, "where did my brother come up with a word like extreme, and how did he know how to use it in a sentence correctly?"

My mom and sister stopped clearing the table, and everyone's eyes, including my dad's, were on me.

"Andy, I don't want you to see that movie," he said.

"But Dad," I pleaded, "I love scary movies, and everyone's going!"

"Everyone but you!" my sister exclaimed.

I couldn't believe it! Now my sister had become my enemy too!

I was speechless. I didn't know what to say. I had to say something! I had to get even with both of them! Without thinking I quickly shouted!

"Chelsea's been texting after ten o'clock, and Lance got home two hours after curfew last Saturday night, but you didn't see it because you were both in bed asleep!"

I did it! I'd beaten my enemies! But by doing so I had also started World War III!

"Chelsea is that true?" my mom asked.

Chelsea was never very good at defending herself. She stumbled, and sputtered, and spewed over every word that came out of her mouth as she tried to defend herself.

"I, well, I, have to, you know, answer, I have to everyone, text them back that..."

She suddenly stopped talking. I could see the blood draining from her head. Her face turned pale and her body started to shake and convulse. Drool dribbled out of the side of her mouth.

"Chelsea, no texting for two days," my mom ordered. "I'll expect your cell phone in my room by bedtime."

My sister let out a gasp and crumpled into a heap of quivering flesh on the floor. She started shaking and convulsing even more. I could tell that the texting withdrawals were already setting in.

I looked at my brother who was giving me a long, cold stare.

"Is that true, Lance?" my dad asked.

Lance never lied, and if he did, and got caught, he took his punishment like a man.

"Lance?"

"Yeah Dad," he said slowly, "I came in two hours late last Saturday."

Lance kept staring me down. I could tell by his look that I was a dead man, but not tonight. Tonight, I had won the battle. I'd be a dead man and meet my fate some other night.

"Then you're grounded from going out this Saturday," my dad stated.

My sister let out a gasp. She reached her arm out toward my brother and barely managed an audible, "Lance," before collapsing back onto the floor.

Lance slowly got out of his chair, his eyes boring into my head like a drill bit drills into wood. He quietly excused himself and walked out of the kitchen.

I knew I had destroyed his Saturday night, and to a teenager, a Saturday night was as valuable as a month's worth of allowance.

"As for you young man..."

"Oh, oh," I thought, "here comes one of my dad's many 'young man' speeches. I had a closet full of them that I've collected over the years."

"I don't want you to see *Carved*. You and your friends can see *I've Got the Ring and You've Got the Finger*. Is that understood?"

"Yes Sir," I said in the most disappointed sound I could muster.

That night I lay awake in bed thinking about the events that had unfolded at dinner. Suddenly an idea popped into my head

"That's it," I thought, "I'll buy a ticket to *I've Got the Ring and You've Got the Finger*, and then I'll sneak into *Carved*!"

There was only one problem with my plan. Lance usually worked at the Cinema Center on Friday nights. He'd be watching to see if I tried to sneak into *Carved* and he'd catch me for sure! I kept thinking.

Suddenly the name Humpy Baxter popped into my head! Humpy Baxter is a guy who goes to the high school across town except he didn't look like a high school kid! He looked like a

45

homeless grownup guy! Humpy Baxter would always hang out at the movie theatre and buy tickets to R rated movies for all of the underage kids. He'd make a huge profit by charging each kid twenty dollars. He would buy their tickets, and then he'd walk into the movie with them, like he was one of their parents! I remember one night I saw him walk into an R rated movie with ten or twenty kids! Seriously! Are the employees at the Cinema Center really that stupid? Did they think he adopted that many kids? Humpy Baxter was my answer.

Dad always gave me twenty dollars when I went to see a movie. It covered the cost of the movie and snacks. I'd just have to do without the snacks. I slowly fell asleep while visions of horror movies danced in my head.

Every student has a subject that they're not very good in. My subject is history. It's not that I don't get it, because I do, it's just that I'm not very interested in it. I know I shouldn't feel that way, that a lot of things have happened in history over the years which allow me to have what I have now. I know that I have freedom, freedom of speech, a good home, and a great family, it's just that I'm here now. I'm a part of history that's happening now. I need to focus on the history that's happening in my life and not what happened a hundred years ago.

As I sat in class I began to think of the classic horror movie *Halloween*. I stared out the window and imagined Michael Myers standing on the playground, a white mask covering his face. My mind began to drift as I started to think of titles of horror movies that I'd like to see made into movies.

The White Room, The Bloody Room, Gangster Vs. Alien.

I looked over at Brad Thompson as he tried to stick his tongue up his nose. I continued thinking of titles.

Brad's Face, Brad's Mom (if you've ever met his mom, you know what I mean,) *The Sad Story of Joseph* (my friend Joe whose cat and dog died on the same day,) *The Scary House, Nightmares Do Come True, Never Fall In Love At First Sight, Killing My Sister, Killing My Brother, The Curfew.*

I snapped out of it for a second and looked around the classroom in a daze. Mr. Paxson was at the front of the room lecturing. I had no idea what he was talking about, so I continued with my thoughts.

The Lecture It'll Bore You To Death, The School, The Last Bell, Two Missed Calls, Haunting In September, The Farmer's Malice, Murder Motel, Frozen, Bloodshot, Scary Night, The Gutters, Deathly Hallows, Stabbed In The Back... By My Brother, The Mean Steak. "The Mean Steak? What the heck?"

"Andy? Andy? Would you like to comment on what Bradley had to say? Andy?" Mr. Paxson asked.

"Huh, what?" I asked.

"Would you like to comment on what Bradley had to say?" he repeated.

"About what?"

The class and all of my friends started to laugh.

"I think you were daydreaming, Andy," Mr. Paxson said.

"Bradley commented on World War II and Hitler. I thought you might want to comment on what he said."

"World War II? Hitler?"

I slowly started to convey my thoughts. Convey, my big grown up word for the day. Convey, it means to communicate, impart, make known.

I heard a few more chuckles around the classroom.

Mr. Paxson stared at me.

"If Hitler were in a horror movie, he could be compared to Michael Myers from *Halloween*, Freddy Krueger from A *Nightmare on Elm Street*, or Jason Voorhees from *Friday the 13th*." I heard more laughter.

"Thank you, Andy," Mr. Paxson said, stopping my comments dead in their tracks.

"No wait," I thought, "I know where I'm going with this!"

"Could I please finish Mr. Paxson?" I asked. "I really do have a point."

"All right, Andy," Mr. Paxson said leaning over my desk, "you've got one minute."

I started out slowly.

"Europe was the backdrop for a real horror story known as World War II. The victims of this horror story were the Jews and anyone else that stood in Hitler or the Nazi's way. Like the murderers in horror movies, Hitler and his army swept across small towns like Haddonfield, and Crystal Lake. Hitler and his army killed millions of innocent people. Eventually, the evil in

Europe was stopped by the United States and its allies. Good won out over evil, just as it does in most horror movies. Unless there's a sequel or World War III."

Everyone in the room was speechless, including Mr. Paxson.

"It's just a connection," I said. "World War II can be compared to a horror movie, except more people died in World War II."

You could have heard a pin drop as the bell rang.

"We'll continue this conversation in our next class period," Mr. Paxson said. "Class dismissed."

I walked into the hallway where I was immediately surrounded by Kyle Krantz, Jett Bingenheimer, and Grant Fiddler.

"Dude, that was awesome!" Jett Bingenheimer exclaimed, "Mr. Paxson thought he caught you daydreaming and you totally proved him wrong!"

"No way did you compare Michael Myers to Hitler!" exclaimed Kyle Krantz, "that was awesome!"

"So what time do you want to meet at the movie?" asked Grant Fiddler.

"Movie starts at 7:30, let's meet at 6:30," Jett answered.

The Cinema Center was packed! People were everywhere! Both *Carved* and *You've Got the Ring and I've Got the Finger* were selling out.

"Look at all the people!" Kyle Krantz exclaimed.

"We're never going to get into *Carved*," sighed Jett Bimgenheimer.

"Sure we will," Grant Fiddler exclaimed. "We'll buy a ticket to another movie and then we'll sneak in!"

"I already thought of that," I answered, "I'm sure they're checking tickets at the door."

"What are we going to do? I just gotta see *Carved*!" Grant moaned.

I felt someone walk up behind us.

"Did you guys want to see *Carved*?"

I turned and there stood Humpy Baxter.

"Yeah, sure," I answered. "How much is it going to cost us?"

"Twenty bucks each."

I let out a sigh of relief. His price hadn't gone up.

We each gave Humpy Baxter $20.00 and headed for the box office.

"My sons and I would like tickets to see *Carved*," Humpy stated.

"One adult and three children?" the cashier asked, cracking her gum. "That'll be $31.00."

Humpy made a $13.00 profit on each one of our tickets!

We made our way through the crowd and into the theatre. My eyes scanned the lobby for Lance. Fortunately he wasn't taking tickets. I spotted him behind the concession stand lugging buckets of ice and dumping them into the ice bins. Sweat was running down his face and he did not look happy!

My dad had gotten a cold so I didn't have to worry about him catching us. Mr. Brunner had given us a ride to the theatre and Mr. Michelson was going to pick us up so we were covered. All that mattered now was that Humpy got us into the theatre. As we walked across the lobby toward theatre 13, I noticed about twenty-five other kids standing by the entryway.

"Holy crap," I said to myself, "the movie's not the only thing making a killing tonight!"

We got to our seats just as the lights started to go down and the previews began. We saw previews for *Transformers 6, Indiana Jones and the Very Last Crusade, Marley and Me- The Next Litter,* and *High School Musical 5- College Graduation.*

"Wow!" I thought to myself, "why can't the people who make movies come up with any new ideas?"

The "feature presentation, please turn off your cell phones" commercial came on and then it was time for *Carved!*

Carved was better than I could have ever imagined! For two solid hours, arms, legs, heads, and hearts, were flying everywhere, and all in 3-D! The twenty-seven victims were screaming at the top of their lungs as they were knifed, stabbed with pitch forks and machetes, hung from meat hooks, and run over by plows. Including the evil farmer, who died at the end when he fell into his own combine and his body parts sprayed all across his corn field!

When the movie ended and the lights came up, my eyes were as big as Frisbees. I didn't even remember the ride home from the movie theatre! I kept thinking of all of the murder and bloodletting.

As I walked through the front door of my house, I had the shakes. I let out a small gasp as I headed down the hallway thinking that one of the coats on the coat rack was somebody standing in the corner with a butcher's knife.

As I was upstairs brushing my teeth, Lance threw open the bathroom door saying, "Hey jerk face, I didn't see you come out of *I've Got the Ring, You've Got the Finger!*"

"I was there!" I answered.

"Liar," my brother responded, "what was the movie about?"

"It was about a guy," I said slowly, "who wanted to marry a girl, and he had the ring, and she had the finger."

A second passed, and then my brother leaned into me, squinted his eyes, and said, "You didn't see that movie, you saw *Carved!*"

"Did not!"

"Did so!"

"Did not!"

"Did so!"

"Boys!" It was my father, coughing and hacking from his bedroom, "go to bed!"

Lance and I walked out of the bathroom still arguing, but in a whisper.

"Liar!"

"Dictator!"

"Liar!"

"Dictator!

"You better watch your back Andy Wink! Because when I get done with you..."

I slammed the bedroom door shut in my brother's face as he was in the middle of his sentence, and locked the door behind me. I pulled back my Star Wars blanket and sheet, got into bed, turned off the light, and pulled the pillow under my head.

I couldn't sleep. I kept tossing and turning in my bed thinking about Carved. Every little creak in my bedroom scared me. The tree branches outside of my window swayed in the wind and threw scary shadows on my walls that I had never seen before! The shadows danced around my bed like they were going to reach around my neck and strangle me.

I pulled the blanket over my head.

"This is ridiculous!" I whispered to myself under the blanket, "I'm in the sixth grade and I'm acting like a baby! Besides, it's hot under here!"

I threw the blanket off me and decided to go down to the kitchen to fix myself a sandwich. I always get tired after I eat so I figured this was the best solution to help me get back to sleep.

As I was making my sandwich, I heard a noise in the living room.

"Hello?" I asked. I wasn't scared, I was holding a knife, but I was a little nervous because I didn't know who was in the other room.

I finished making my sandwich and then heard another noise come from the living room.

"You gonna sleep all night?" I asked nervously, looking into the living room, "you know what they say. It's the early bird that catches the worm!"

I looked into the darkness of the living room to see who was there.

"Andy," a voice answered from the darkness, "it's three o'clock in the morning, the worm is still in bed!"

I shrugged my shoulders.

"So I like to get a head start on the day. Do you want a sandwich? "

There was a pause as I waited for an answer.

"I said do you want a sandwich?" I asked impatiently.

There was still no answer. I walked into the living room.

"Who's out here? Lance if you're trying to scare me..."

I turned on the living room lights, and looked around, nothing. I walked back into the kitchen to find a strange looking man, dressed in a black cloak, sitting at the kitchen table. A sickle leaned against the chair next to him.

"It's not Lance, Andy, and yes, I'd love a sandwich."

I was scared, but I didn't run. Was I dreaming, sleepwalking? My curiosity had gotten the best of me.

"Who are you?" I asked.

"I'm Death. Do you have any other kind of bread besides whole grain?"

"That's the only bread we have. Mom says that white bread's not good for you. What do you mean you're Death?" I asked.

"I'm Death. The grim reaper, blah, blah, blah, I'm here to talk to you."

"About what?" I asked, "If this has anything to do with that time I took my sister's favorite doll and blew it up in the microwave, I was only 7 years old! I didn't know right from wrong!"

"It doesn't have anything to do with that," Death said, shaking his finger at me, "although that was a very mean thing to do."

"Hey, you've got bones for fingers!" I exclaimed.

"Makes for a better effect," Death answered, "sandwich please."

"Not until you tell me why you're here," I answered nervously, folding my arms over my chest.

"I told you," Death said slowly, "I want to talk to you."

"Look, it can't be my time yet," I said in disbelief, "I'm only twelve."

"I've taken children younger than you, Andy."

"That's not a very nice thing to say!" I responded, pointing my finger at Death.

"It's true," Death replied, "I don't discriminate."

This scared me. I was hoping that if this was a dream I'd wake up, and if it wasn't a dream, my parents would wake up when they heard me in the kitchen.

"Andy, there's nothing to be afraid of."

"Oh yeah," I stated, a little more bravely, "how would you like it if you got up in the middle of the night, went into your kitchen to fix a sandwich, and some guy in a black cloak, with boney fingers, and a sickle's sitting at your kitchen table?"

"It's a scythe."

"A what?" I asked.

"It's a scythe, not a sickle. It's an agricultural hand tool used for mowing grass, or it could be used for reaping crops."

"So why do you carry it around with you?"

"Again, it's for an effect. It's the way you see me."

Death reached across the table and slid the sandwich toward him. He took a bite.

"Hey, this sandwich is delicious! What kind is it?"

"Peanut butter," I answered.

"Could I have a glass of milk please?"

"First answer my question. Why are you here?" I asked.

"I wanted to talk with you about this obsession that you have with me, and horror movies."

I paused for a second and then poured Death a glass of milk.

"Yoda," he said looking disgusted at the Star Wars glass I handed him, "I prefer Darth Vader."

"That glass broke," I answered.

"Andy, have a seat," he said patting the chair next to him.

"I'll sit over here if you don't mind."

I sat in a chair on the opposite side of the table. I stared at Death, not knowing what to say. He took another bite of his sandwich and chased it with a drink of milk.

"Why do you like horror movies?" Death asked.

"Is this a trick question?" I thought to myself.

"I like to be scared?" I answered slowly.

"Are you scared now?" Death asked.

"Should I be?"

"Maybe... do you always answer every question with a question?"

"Do you?"

"You're a clever boy Andy, a very clever boy."

Death took another bite of his sandwich.

"So what's your favorite horror movie?"

"Are you kidding?" I asked.

"Question with a question again," Death said wagging a boney finger at me.

"Well," I thought, "There are so many that I like. I like *The Omen.*"

"He's a bad little boy..." Death commented.

"I love *The Exorcist!*" I exclaimed.

"Bad little girl..." Death commented again.

"I like *Psycho...*" I said.

"Bad big boy... and girl," Death answered chuckling. "What else?"

"I like the *Nightmare on Elm Street* movies and all of the

Halloween movies both the old ones and the remakes, except for *Halloween 3*. That was so bad it was scary!"

I laughed at my joke as Death finished his sandwich.

"Those movies are all R rated. How do you get to watch them?"

"I stay up late, catch them on one of the movie channels."

"Don't your parents know about the Parental Control Lock on your cable box? What about *Carved*? That wasn't playing on a movie channel? How did you see that movie?"

"I snuck in with some friends."

Suddenly I felt guilty.

"Do you have a bathroom?" Death asked.

"Uh, yeah, it's through there," I said pointing in the direction of the living room, "I didn't know that you..."

"That Death uses the bathroom?" he interrupted.

I laughed, "If you gotta go, you gotta go, right?"

Death got up from the kitchen table and walked toward the bathroom.

"I noticed you have Wii Sports Golf" he said, "why don't you start it up? I'll use my "sickle" for a club."

Death laughed as he walked into the bathroom.

I sat down on the couch, turned on my Wii game system and pressed A on the Wii-mote. I chose Wii Sports on the menu. I heard the toilet flush and the bathroom door open.

"Hey Death," I said, "I don't think you can use your scythe on a Wii system, I don't think the game system will recognize it."

I suddenly felt the cold blade of the scythe on my neck.

"Well how about a close-shave then?"

I looked up and saw the evil farmer from *Carved* standing above me. I felt the blade cutting into my neck. I let out the loudest scream I could, and then, I woke up screaming, tossing and turning at the foot of my parents' bed.

"Andy! Andy! Wake up!" my dad shouted as he shook me. I woke up shaking and whimpering in my dad's arms.

"Oh hi Dad," I said looking into my dad's eyes, "I was having a really bad dream!"

"Andy? Why were you sleeping at the foot of our bed?" my mom asked.

"I was afraid," I answered.

"Andy," my mom said, "you're drenched in sweat! I'm going to get you another pair of pajamas."

My mom left the room and went across the hall to my bedroom. My dad looked at me with a concerned look on his face.

"You went to that movie, didn't you?" my dad asked.

I didn't have to answer, my dad already knew. Parents have a way of figuring things out.

"There's a reason those movies are rated R, Andy," my dad said as he got up and paced the floor. "They're too violent for twelve year old kids!"

"I know Dad," I said staring at the floor.

"But you and your friends snuck in and watched it, didn't you?"

59

I could tell that my dad was upset.

"You and your friends broke a lot of rules tonight, Andy!"

"I know, Dad," I said as my eyes darted around the room looking for Death or the evil farmer, "I know..."

My dad knelt beside me.

"You're still afraid aren't you Andy?"

"Yeah, Dad, I'm scared."

"Don't you see what that movie has done to you Andy? You don't even feel safe in your own house, do you?"

"No Dad."

"I know you're afraid, Andy," my dad said as he hugged me, "I'm going to make sure that you're safe," he whispered.

It took me a couple of weeks before I could fall asleep in my own bed and feel safe again. I kept waking up in the middle of the night screaming, shaking, in a cold sweat.

My dad was really patient with me. When I woke up in the middle of the night, we'd talk, and they were some of the best talks we ever had!

We talked about my bad dreams.

We talked about Death, and about how when someone dies how they're missed by their family and friends.

We talked about how I would never have to feel like I was alone, that Mom and Dad would always be there for me.

We talked about why movies are rated R, and how kids my age shouldn't watch R rated movies because R rated movies are rated R for a reason, and that reason's usually violence.

We talked about movies and video games and about how the characters are always shooting each other and never getting hurt. We talked about how if someone were shot in real life, they'd be hurt or even die.

But most important of all, we talked about my punishment and about how long I would be grounded.

Two weeks later was Halloween but I wouldn't be trick or treating. Dad had grounded me for four weeks. Not only was I grounded from Halloween and trick or treating, but my punishment also included going directly to school in the morning and coming straight home when school was done. I wasn't allowed to play with my friends, I wasn't allowed to watch TV or DVDs, I could only read or write which was okay, because you know how I like to write!

On Halloween night, I was looking out my window and watching the trick or treaters run from house to house filling their bags full of candy, when suddenly my bedroom door flew open.

"Hey loser!"

It was my brother Lance.

"What do you think of my costume?" he asked, as he walked around the room showing off his costume.

My brother was dressed in a black robe, with a hood, and he was carrying a scythe.

"You're Death," I said in disbelief.

"That's right," he said as he put his hand on my shoulder.

"And you've got bones for fingers," I continued.

"That's right," he answered, "they're just plastic bones on sticks that I hold under my sleeves. It makes for a better effect!"

Lance shot me a wicked grin as he leaned over and whispered in my ear.

"I told you to watch your back!"

I couldn't believe it. My brother had won World War III.

"Lance," my dad said, as he walked into my bedroom, "are you ready? Your mom and sister are waiting downstairs."

"Ready Dad!" Lance shouted, as he ran out of my bedroom.

"You going to be okay staying home alone on Halloween?" my dad asked.

"I'll be fine," I answered, trying not to show my disappointment.

"You sure?" my dad asked.

"Yeah, I'm going to write."

"Well your mom's got a bowl of candy downstairs on the table by the front door for the trick or treaters."

A few seconds of silence passed. I could tell my dad felt bad, because I felt bad.

"Next year, huh Pal?"

"Sure Dad, next year," I answered.

I followed my dad downstairs and watched out the front door as my family began their journey of trick or treating and disappeared into the darkness.

I noticed the colorful leaves roll across the front yard. The air had gotten colder. Fall was my favorite season of the year. I loved the colors, and the smell of burning leaves, the cold night air, football, and Halloween. Not only did I love Halloween because it was Halloween, but I loved Halloween because it was the beginning of the big holidays, Halloween, Thanksgiving, and Christmas!

A ghost and a goblin ran up to the front door.

"Trick or treat!" they both shouted.

I held out the bowl of candy. They each grabbed a handful, turned, and ran down the sidewalk. I closed the front door grabbed my composition book and pencil, and began to write. My thoughts flowed out so fast on the paper my hand had trouble keeping up with them...

James Gunn's new horror movie Carved starts tomorrow at the Cinema Center, and I, Andy Wink, **will be one of the first ones in line to see it...**

The Housesitter

5. Ms. Rife, my fourth grade teacher, asked me to housesit for a week over Christmas break, and I Andy Wink was up for the job!

Ms. Rife was one of the best teachers I'd ever had! She always made every school day a lot of fun!

You know how sometimes you get a teacher who thinks that you're in school to learn, and that learning isn't supposed to be fun? Well, Ms. Rife made learning fun! When I had her as a teacher, she had a caring attitude, she wanted to make a difference in our lives, and as a class, she had high expectations of us. She was always prepared and organized, and she always engaged the class and made things interesting and fun! There it is my big word for the day, engaged. Engaged means to make things interesting, engage the class, make us ask the "why" question! You know? Make us look at all sides of everything as we learn!

I remember when I had Ms. Rife in class. I liked her so much that I made her a little ceramic plaque in art class. The plaque read...

Ms. Rife

Loves her kids

Always has a smile

Inspires knowledge

Helps me to become a better person

with each discovery
Is understanding
Has a smart brain
Tells me I can do it
Likes to laugh
Shows me that she cares

Yup, Ms. Rife is one of the best teachers out there and over Christmas break she was going to London with her husband Ed and she asked me to housesit!

She said that Christmas in London would be like something out of Dickens. I'm not sure what she meant by that, but I think it had something to do with A *Christmas Carol* by Charles Dickens. My family had gone to see A *Christmas Carol* at the Denver Center and I knew that it took place in London, so I think that's what she meant.

Now I know what you're thinking. A sixth grader? By himself? House sitting? For a week? Over Christmas break? It's true! Ms. Rife only lived six houses down from ours and Dad said it would be okay. He said that he'd "check in on me from time to time" to make sure I was doing okay. And Ms. Rife was going to pay me $150.00 which is a lot of money for a kid!

Ms. Rife also had three cats and she said she wanted someone to stay at the house so the cats would be in their own living environment. One cat was named Jack. Jack is black, so I thought Jack Black (I always try to make some connection to help me remember names.) Charlie is an orange kitten so I thought breakfast orange juice to help me remember his name. Benny is a white older cat. To help me remember his name, I thought of Benny's restaurant which is a really great Mexican restaurant in Denver!

Dad dropped me off at Ms. Rife's house on the first Friday of Christmas break. I was excited! Christmas break, a week of house sitting, and then a week of vacation, video games, and movies! But best of all, no school!

"Boy it's hot out!" my dad exclaimed, "Indian summer!"

"Indian summer?" I asked, as I unloaded the car. "What's Indian summer?"

"Indian summer's a day like today, a hot day. It usually happens in November or sometimes later," he answered, "after the leaves have fallen from the trees."

I wiped the sweat from my forehead.

"It must be nearly sixty degrees!" my dad exclaimed. "It sure doesn't feel like December!"

Dad carried my suitcase through the front door and into the guest room.

"I'll help you unpack," he said.

"Dad, I'm twelve years old, I can unpack my own suitcase!"

"Okay," he answered, "I'll go out to the car and get your coat and gloves. The weather report said that it's going to get colder later on in the week."

Dad headed out to the car as I walked into the kitchen. A

cat darted in front of me.

"Here kitty, kitty, kitty."

The cat stopped, looked at me, and then ran into the living room.

I noticed a note from Ms. Rife lying on the counter. I started to read it.

Hi Andy!

Ed's Cell 303-506-8433

My Cell 303-506-8431

You probably won't be able to get a hold of us at either one of these numbers because we'll be in London so call your Dad.

Emergency Cat Clinic 303-875-7387

The refrigerator and freezer are filled with food, help yourself!

I opened the refrigerator and freezer and they were filled with my favorite foods! Hamburgers, hot dogs, a ham for ham sandwiches, chocolate milk, orange juice, frozen pizzas, Bagel Bites, Pizza Rolls, ice cream, and on the counter bread, macaroni and cheese mix, spaghetti and spaghetti sauce, cereal, apples, bananas, and a chocolate cake!

"Wow," I exclaimed, "there's enough food to last me all winter!"

I continued with Ms. Rife's note.

In the morning, after the cats wake you up: One small can of food from the pantry. Split in two cat dishes. Jack usually isn't interested, if he is, put some food in the little Chinese dish.

I looked around the counter for the little Chinese dish. I found it next to the refrigerator with a Post-it note on it that read, "little Chinese dish."

You could tell Ms. Rife was a teacher. Her note was very detailed. I continued to read.

There's deli chicken in the fridge meat drawer that Charlie loves torn into small pieces- you can give him treats of that in the little Chinese dish, whenever.

Please give the cats fresh water, with ice cubes from the fridge. I know, I know, they're spoiled.

You don't have to let the cats out in the a.m. unless you want to. Jack likes to go out on the front porch. When he returns the first time, keep them all in the house. Bond with Jack a little before you let him out and you may have to "sweet talk" him in.

Charlie beats up on Benny, yell at him and he'll back off!

The paper should be delivered each morning. Please put the papers on the kitchen counter.

Squirrel duty. Please go to the side of the yard in the morning and feed the squirrels. There's one that always hangs out by the garage. I call him Chip. One cup of squirrel mix, layered with peanuts on top of the big bowl by the shed. I know, I know, I'm a freak! If you play in the yard, let the kitties join you. Chip will entertain Charlie and not bug you for more food. If Jack leaves the backyard, check on him periodically on the front porch and let him in.

Charlie can never leave the backyard! He doesn't try, twice he's run up a fence chasing Chip, but it's rare. He loves the toy with the feather attached.

I looked across the counter and next to the little Chinese bowl was a Post-it note pointing to a stick with a feather on it. The Post-it note read, "stick with feather."

I continued to read.

Charlie loves that toy with the feather and he'll drag it around. If you play with him in the back yard or the house, he'll be very happy!

At night, kitties never go out after dark. Bring them in before dark or Jack will take off.

Under the Christmas tree in the living room is a present for you that you may not open until Christmas Day!

Thank you, thank you, a million thank yous! We'll see you next week!

I looked in the living room and underneath the Christmas tree was a gift wrapped in beautiful wrapping paper with a red bow on it. The tag underneath the bow read: To Andy from Ms. Rife. I put the present to my ear and shook it as my dad walked through the front door.

"One snowsuit, one set of gloves, and one coat. You're set Pal! You gonna be okay?"

"Yeah, Ms. Rife left me a note on what to do. You can tell she's a teacher because it's a very detailed note. She left me a Christmas present too. She said not to open it until Christmas day."

"That was nice of her. How are you set for food?"

"The refrigerator's full," I answered.

"All right then! You sure you don't want me to help you unpack?"

I gave my dad the "are you kidding me" look.

"All right then," he said, "I've got some last minute Christmas shopping to do so give me a call if you need anything, all right Andy?"

"I will Dad."

I watched through the front window as my dad pulled away in the car and then I walked into the living room.

There were more notes. Ms. Rife had photo copied all of the remote controls.

Yo! I'm the TV remote.

She had arrows pointing to the different buttons.

On and Off.
Volume.

Don't use this button for channels.

Use this button to pick the DVD player and go back to TV. First punch input button, press arrow down to switch to DVD player. Switch back to get TV.

I went to the next photo copy.

Howdy! I'm the DVD remote. Use the TV remote first to switch to DVD.

The last photo copy read.

Hi! I'm the Comcast remote. Use me to change channels. Use these buttons to choose On Demand. See Comcast guide for HD Channel information. Do not use me for on and off or volume.

Did I understand all of the remote notes? You bet I did! Whenever the remotes get messed up at my house, who do my parents call to figure them out? Me. I'm a kid and that's what kids learn these days, modern technology.

I unpacked, fed the cats, and fixed myself a yummy cheese pizza. After doing the dishes, I was anxious to watch TV. Both

How the Grinch Stole Christmas and *Rudolph the Red-Nosed Reindeer* were on.

As I watched the Grinch, I thought to myself, why is the Grinch so unhappy? What made him so unhappy that he felt like he had to commit burglary? Did he have a terrible childhood? Was he unhappy because he didn't have a girlfriend and only lived with a dog that he dressed like a reindeer? And yeah, I realize that at the end of the show that his heart grew a bunch of sizes and made him a nice Grinch, but that still didn't change the fact that he probably got ten years in jail for stealing the Who's property.

Rudolph the Red-Nosed Reindeer was on after The Grinch except on a different channel. Rudolph also made me think. I thought to myself that a Christmas show like Rudolph couldn't be made today. There's too much bullying in the show. Remember how the coach and the other reindeer wouldn't let Rudolph play in any reindeer games? That wouldn't happen today. No Child Left Behind. Teachers and coaches would make sure that every reindeer got to play in the reindeer games.

When Rudolph was over, the news came on and a weather report flashed across the bottom of the screen, "Blizzard warning, high wind advisory, record low temperatures." I didn't pay much attention to the weather forecast because I was thinking of other parts of movies that bothered me.

The Wizard of Oz. My favorite movie of all time! But at the end, before Dorothy gets ready to hop a hot air balloon, she tells the Scarecrow that she'll probably miss him most of all. How do you think that made the Tin Man and the Cowardly Lion feel? Sad.

Harry Potter. The books were a great read and the movies are amazing, but think about it. There's too much drama at the Hogwarts School, not to mention danger. When I go to school, I want to learn, do my work, after school go to baseball practice, and then come home. I don't want to have to worry about the possibility of getting murdered by one of my back stabbing classmates!

The phone rang. I answered it. It was my dad.

"How's it going Pal, is the stove off?"

"Yeah Dad, I made a pizza and then turned it off."

"What are you up to?" he asked.

Yawning I said, "I just finished watching The Grinch and Rudolph and now I'm going to watch *Home Alone* on TBS."

"Sounds like a plan. Listen Pal, I don't know what you have to do outside tomorrow for Ms. Rife, but there's supposed to be a blizzard and the wind chill's going to be around ten below."

I immediately thought of Chip.

"So if the weather forecast's right, and Channel 9's been known to be wrong, but if there's a blizzard, I want you to stay inside. Got it?"

"Got it," I sighed.

I heard my mom yell in the background, "Tell him to call if he gets lonely!"

"Your mom says to call if you get lonely."

"I heard her. I think the whole neighborhood heard her. I'll be fine," I answered.

"I know you will. Give us a call if you need anything, okay Pal?"

"Okay Dad."

I hung up the phone, put on my jacket, and stepped outside into the dark backyard.

A light on the back patio turned on.

"Cool," I thought, "motion sensor lights!"

I ran across the backyard, grabbed Chip's black plastic feeding bowl, the squirrel mix, the bag of peanuts, and ran back to the porch. I set everything inside by the porch door.

I took off my coat, hung it up on a coat rack, and snuggled up on the couch with three blankets over me watching *Home Alone*. Again, I began to think.

I thought to myself if Harry and Marv, the "Wet Bandits" in *Home Alone*, were shot with a gun, slipped on icy stairs, were hit in the face with an iron, were burned by a door knob, stepped on a nail, got their heads burned by a blow torch, stepped on ornaments barefoot, were hit in the face with paint cans, tripped on a trip wire, were hit in the chest with a crow bar, swung into a brick wall, and then got hit in the head with a snow shovel, I think they would have ended up in the hospital with broken bones and a concussion, or even died. But if that would have happened, the movie wouldn't have been as funny.

I also thought about how cool it was that Kevin McAllister and the neighborhood snow shovel guy became friends. If my dad was right about the weather, and he usually was, our neighborhood would need a lot of snow shovel guys after the blizzard ended.

I fell asleep as the wind outside began to roar and the snow began to swirl.

I woke up and Charlie was sitting on my chest. He was licking chocolate off his mouth and paws.

"Oh no," I thought.

I looked out the window and the entire world was white. As far as I could see, white, and the snow was still falling, and the wind was still howling!

I walked into the kitchen figuring the cats were hungry. There was chocolate cake everywhere, on the counter, on the floor, in the sink. There were chocolate paw prints all over the kitchen! The cats must have had a field day with the cake because it took me over an hour to clean it all up!

After feeding the cats, I went to the back door to feed Chip. I opened the door and was almost knocked over by the force of the wind and the snow! The snow was as high as the door knob! I closed the door, put the squirrel food and peanuts in the black plastic feeding dish, and dug a small opening in the snow by the door so that it wouldn't blow away.

I closed the door shivering. I decided to take a shower to warm up.

After my shower I sat in the living room with the cats and stared out the window. I noticed that the wind was blowing over little footprints in the snow. I got up and went to the back porch door. I opened it and saw that Chip had eaten his breakfast. Seed and peanut shells were everywhere! Chip wasn't a very neat eater! I looked out across the snow, but didn't see him. I fought the wind pushing against the door as I tried to close it.

The telephone rang. It was my dad.

"Is the stove off?" he asked, as I answered the telephone.

"I haven't used the stove today," I answered.

"How about this snow, Pal?" my dad asked, "There must be three foot drifts out there!"

"It's up to the doorknob on the back door here," I answered.

"Well don't go outside, you understand Andy?"

"I won't Dad," I answered.

"Tell him to call if he gets lonely!" my mom screamed in the background.

"And tell him to call if a murderer's trying to break into the house and slit his throat!" my brother Lance yelled in the background.

"Your Mother said to call if you get lonely," my dad said, "and Lance said hello."

Suddenly the walls of the house shook and the wind shrieked. The phone went dead. I was cut off from the outside world.

The cats and I spent most of the day taking naps and staring out the window. It just kept snowing, and snowing, and snowing! I'd never seen snow drifts so high!

Later that night, *Christmas Vacation* was on TBS. I loved that movie and no matter how many times I'd seen it, I always laughed out loud. I especially liked the part when the squirrel jumped out of the Christmas tree and chased everyone in the Griswold living room. Ms. Rife's cats meowed loudly and then ran away from the TV when the Griswold's cat got electrocuted under the Christmas tree. Maybe animals really do know what's happening when they watch TV. I think there have been studies made on that somewhere.

The wind continued to howl and the snow was now creeping over the windowsill.

I woke up the next morning and my nose was cold. There was a strange feeling in my ears. I peeked out from underneath my blanket and looked out the bedroom window. The blizzard was over. I jumped out of bed and the air was cold. The heat was working, but it was still cold. It must have been very cold outside!

I went to the telephone. No dial tone.

I opened the back porch door and the snow was as high as my head. The sky was bright blue and the snow glistened. I closed the door and wondered where the cats were. I walked into the living room and saw all three cats sitting in front of the fireplace, mesmerized! There it was, my big word for the day, mesmerized. It means to hold your attention, like you're under a spell.

I moved toward the fireplace to see what they were staring at.

On the other side of the fireplace glass sat Chip, eating a peanut. He wasn't the least bit afraid of the cats even though they were licking their lips.

"What the heck?" I said to myself, as I slowly walked toward the fireplace.

The cats looked up at me, and then back at Chip.

"How did you? What are you doing? I guess it's a good thing that I didn't start a fire last night." I was at a loss of words.

I fed the cats and went back to the fireplace. At first I didn't see Chip. I pushed my nose against the glass, but I didn't see him! Maybe he'd gone back up the chimney? Suddenly, out of nowhere, Chip lowered himself slowly; he was upside down on the other side of the glass. He let out a small squeak. He turned right side up and tried to run up the chimney. He fell down on to the middle of the fireplace.

"Chip's stuck," I thought, "What can I do to help him?"

Chip squeaked again. He threw his empty peanut shell down and stared at me. I figured he was hungry.

I went to the porch door and picked up Chip's bowl. I filled it with food and walked to the fireplace. I slowly started to open one of the fireplace doors. Chip scurried up the chimney and then fell back down. He backed up as I put his bowl in the fireplace. I closed the fireplace door.

Chip started to eat and he looked very happy.

I put on my snowsuit and decided to go outside and look around.

I stepped out the back porch door, realizing the snow was so high that I'd have to climb out over the snow that surrounded the door and hopefully walk on top of the snow drifts which had been hardened by the wind.

I stood on a snow drift looking across the yard. I must have been eight feet tall! Everything was white; the trees and the rooftops. Smoke was coming out of the chimneys from the houses around me and billowing up into the sky. Not a car was moving on the streets.

The snow drift that I was standing on reached all of the way to Ms. Rife's roof. I walked along the drift and sat on the roof. I figured I'd be safe. If I slipped and fell, I figured I'd just fall a few feet into a big pile of snow.

What a view! I could see our house from here! I wondered what my family was doing. I looked up at the chimney and wondered how Chip had gotten down it.

I carefully climbed up to the chimney and noticed that part of the screen had blown away. I tried to figure out a way to help Chip climb out.

Suddenly, the sunshine gave way to darkness. I looked toward the north as black clouds started to roll toward me.

I slid off the roof and made my way to the back porch door.

Just as I reached it, the wind and blowing snow hit! Another blizzard! It took all of my strength to pull open the door and stumble inside.

After feeding the cats, and Chip, I lay on the couch wondering how long this storm would last. I also wondered how I was going to help Chip. I thought of the fable, *The Ant and the Dove* by Aesop. Ms. Rife had taught us this fable in the fourth grade.

The fable was about a dove that saves an ant and the same ant saves the dove. The ant falls into a river and is swept downstream. The dove drops a branch into the river which the ant grabs onto and then guides himself to shore. A hunter points his gun at the dove to shoot him and the ant bites the hunter in the foot causing the hunter to miss the dove. One good deed deserves another as they say.

I kept wondering how I could help Chip.

After a few minutes I sat up and shouted, "That's it! Just like the movie *Home Alone*, all I needed was some rope!"

I thought about how the Wet Bandits had swung on a piece of rope and crashed into the brick wall of the house. All I needed was a long piece of rope to lower down the chimney so that Chip could climb out.

I went into the garage and looked around. The Rifes were outdoors people. They hiked and mountain climbed and went camping. It didn't take me long to find a piece of rope that would work. I grabbed it and went into the living room to plan

Chip's escape.

Chip and Ms. Rife's cats watched with great interest. About every foot I tied the rope into a knot. I figured the knots would give Chip something to hold onto so that he could just scurry out of the chimney. When I finished, I looked out of the window and sighed. The blizzard was still roaring.

After dinner and pet feeding, The *Sound of Music* was on TV. The Sound of Music's a great movie, but again, my brain went into overdrive and looked for flaws in the movie. I mean, sure *The Sound of Music's* got great songs, it makes you feel good, it's set before WWII, the Von Trapp kids get Mary Poppins as their mom, but what about the ending? Sure the Von Trapps hiked across the mountains to Switzerland, without supplies I might add, but what about the nuns in the abbey? What happened to them? I'm guessing they were punished for messing up the Nazi's cars.

I lay on the couch and thought about my family. I wondered what they were doing. Lance was probably playing video games and more than likely Chelsea was texting or tweeting her friends. Mom was probably in the kitchen baking Christmas cookies, and Dad was more than likely in the living room building a fire in the fireplace. I got up and checked the phone again. Still no dial tone. As I fell asleep I started to feel lonely, and I realized that I missed my family.

I woke up in the morning, again with a strange feeling in my ears. The blizzard had stopped! I had breakfast, fed the pets, put on my snowsuit, and went outside carrying the rope. The blizzard that had just ended had changed the way the drifts were in the backyard, but I was still able to walk on one that took me directly to the roof.

I slowly lowered the rope down the chimney. I heard Chip scurrying below. I sat and waited.

"What are you doing up there?" I heard a voice ask.

It was my dad and he was wearing snow shoes!

"What are you doing down there?" I asked, happy to see him.

"Merry Christmas!" my dad said.

"Merry Christmas?" I thought. I'd forgotten all about Christmas with the blizzards and Chip's dilemma.

"Merry Christmas!" I answered cheerfully.

"What are you doing up there?" my dad repeated.

"The chimney screen came loose, and Chip, Ms. Rife's squirrel got stuck in the chimney," I explained, as I crawled off the roof and onto a drift, "I lowered a rope down the chimney with knots in it so he could get out."

"Well aren't you clever?" my dad answered, "What do you say we go to our house and open presents?"

"Yes," I exclaimed!

Dad had brought an extra pair of snow shoes with him. I put them on and we headed toward our house.

"Wait!" I shouted. "Ms. Rife's Christmas present!"

I took off my snow shoes, ran inside, grabbed the present

from underneath the tree, and put it in my coat pocket.

When we got to our house, my mom gave me a big hug!

"Oh, I missed you, Merry Christmas!"

"Merry Christmas, Mom!" I answered.

"Merry Christmas loser!" my brother Lance said as he passed me in the hallway smacking me in the back of my head. We opened our presents in the living room by the Christmas tree, and I got everything that I'd asked for! Tons of DVDs and Wii video games, money from my grandpa, and a Sing and Swoon Justin Bieber Doll... Just kidding! I just wanted to see if you were paying attention.

Later that afternoon, Mom had made the best Christmas dinner ever!

We had (and I had to ask her what everything was so that I could tell you) chestnut soup, a mixed green salad with red-wine and Dijon vinaigrette, baked ham with cherry pomegranate glaze, roast turkey with sage butter and gravy, bourbon sweet potato and apple casserole with a pecan crust, broccoli (which I didn't eat, because I refuse to eat any vegetable that's green), mashed potatoes, and flaky buttermilk biscuits. For dessert we had a choice of pumpkin or apple pie, or a chocolate roulade with raspberry filling (I had to ask Mom about that one too.)

As we were finishing our desert, my dad asked, "Andy, did you open Ms. Rife's present?"

"I forgot!" I said, running to the coat rack.

I reached inside my coat pocket and pulled out my present. I slowly opened it as I walked into the dining room.

Inside was a box, and inside the box was a beautiful writing journal and I have to stress, it's a journal, and not a diary! I opened it up and on the inside flap Ms. Rife had written...

To one of the best writers I know, you get it!

"You get it," I thought to myself, "I wonder what she means by that?"

"What do you suppose she means by that?" I asked my dad.

"Why don't you ask her when she comes home, she'll be home in a few days."

After dinner I bundled up and my dad walked me back to Ms. Rife's house. We walked into the living room and I looked into the fireplace. Chip was gone. I was happy, but I was also a little sad. I wanted Chip to be free, but I also wanted to be close to him, even though I knew that wild animals needed to be in the wild.

Dad fixed the chimney screen and headed home. As I walked inside the house, I noticed dark gray clouds rolling quickly across the sky. I got inside just as another blizzard hit! After feeding the cats, I spent the night drinking hot chocolate, and staring out the window at the snow, thinking about what a wonderful Christmas it had been. I wondered what Ms. Rife was doing in London (probably sleeping, since they were eight hours ahead of us), and I wondered what my friends and families were doing and if they'd had a Christmas as wonderful as I'd had. I also thought about Chip and I wondered if he had a family somewhere.

When Ms. Rife got home from London, I asked her what she meant by "I get it."

She said that it was remarkable that at my age that I "get life." I get what's important and what isn't. I "get" what's right and what's wrong, and I "get" how important my family and friends are.

But most of all, I "get" how to live and care about the things around me, like animals and people. When it comes to animals and people, I always try and do good, kind of like the fable The Ant and the Dove. I've always thought that there are so many possibilities that come from doing good things, and that a good turn is like doing something healthy.

One cold night at the beginning of January, I spent the night writing in my new journal. I wrote some New Years Haikus, a short story about a snowman who comes to life and goes on a three state killing spree (I know, I know, horror stories again,) and I wrote a really great story about a sixth grade boy who house sits for a neighbor and all of the responsibilities that come with that job. That story is called The Housesitter.

My Grandpa

6. It was games night at the Wink house, and I Andy Wink was going to beat everyone at Monopoly!

"You're going down," I said to my brother Lance!

"No way loser! Once a loser, always a loser," Lance responded.

As we were setting up the board and shuffling the cards, the phone rang.

"I'll get it," my mom said, as she left the table.

My brother picked the race car, my sister the dog, my dad chose the cannon, he picked out the thimble for my mom, and I was the battleship.

"I get to be the banker," Lance said.

"Dad can be the banker," I answered. "You cheat."

My brother threw me a look.

Dad started to count out the money as Mom walked back into the room. She looked pale and had a worried look on her face.

"Dan," she started, "it's your father."

My heart suddenly sank. I knew something terrible had happened and I was right. My grandpa had died.

The closest airport we could get the "grievance fare" to was Midway airport in Chicago, Illinois. For those of you that don't know what a "grievance fare" is, it's where the airline gives your family a cheaper flight so that you can go to the funeral of someone in your family. It wasn't my big word for the day, I didn't have one. I was too upset about my grandpa. We would land in Chicago, my grandpa's funeral was in Iowa, three hours away, and we'd have to rent a car to get us there.

As the plane started to land, I looked out the window as the shadow of the plane skipped across the houses below. I thought to myself, "The houses look so small. They look like houses on a Monopoly board."

After we landed, we picked up our luggage from the luggage claim. Everyone's bag was there except for Chelsea's.

"Oh no," Chelsea sighed.

"We'll find it," my mom exclaimed.

"We'll meet you at the car rental desk," my dad said to my mom, as she and Chelsea headed off to the airline counter.

There was a mob of people at the car rental desk as my dad, Lance, and I got in line.

"What's going on?" my dad asked the man in front of us.

"They're out of cars," the man answered.

My heart sank. It was two o'clock and my grandpa's visitation was at seven o'clock. It would take us at least three hours to drive to my grandpa's hometown, which would only leave us a couple of hours to check into our hotel and get cleaned up. A couple of hours, if we got a car!

"Lance, you and Andy wait here in line," my dad said. "I'm going to check the other car rentals to see if they have a car."

Lance and I waited in line for what seemed like forever!

The line hardly moved! Fifteen minutes went by, and then thirty minutes!

"Way to go loser," my brother exclaimed!

"What?" I asked.

"You know this is your fault!"

"My fault," I asked, "how is this my fault?"

"I don't know," Lance answered, "but I'm sure it is!"

I could tell that my brother was upset and that he was just giving me the business. I didn't take what he said personally. I knew this wasn't my fault. I was only twelve years old and I couldn't even drive!

Lance got out his cell phone, looked at a sign sitting on the counter, and began to dial. After a couple of minutes he got through to someone on the other end.

"Uh, yes," he started, "my name's Dan Wink and I'm having trouble picking up a car."

I couldn't believe it! Lance was pretending to be my dad! And he was doing a good job at it!

"Midway," Lance continued.

This is what I loved about my brother! When things got tough, the tough get going, but not my brother. He's one of the toughest! He always steps up to the plate and solves the problem!

After a few minutes Lance got through to a manager.

"Uh yes, this is Dan Wink and I'm at Midway airport with

my family and we're waiting on a car."

I leaned in toward Lance to listen in on the conversation.

"I'm sorry Sir," a man on the other end said, "there are no cars available at this time."

"I understand that," Lance continued, "but I need to tell you something. My father died and we're waiting on a car so that we can drive to his visitation."

Lance's voice cracked. I looked up at him and there were tears coming out of his eyes.

"Yeah, I'll hold," he said, wiping away his tears.

I couldn't believe it! My brother was starting to cry! I didn't know if he was upset about the rental car or loosing Grandpa. I think it was both. Lance leaned into me.

"If you ever tell anyone you saw me crying," Lance said, "I'll kick your butt!"

Lance hit me hard in the arm and moved out of the line.

I stayed in line and rubbed my arm.

I thought to myself, "Why couldn't I cry?"

My grandpa had died three days ago and sure, I felt sad, but I hadn't cried. I caught Chelsea crying a few days ago, and I could tell that Mom and Dad were sad, so why couldn't I cry?

"Well, there's not a car to be had in the entire airport," my dad said as he walked toward me.

"Lance is talking to someone on his cell phone," I said, motioning toward my brother.

A voice came over the intercom.

"Mr. Wink, please come to the courtesy counter," the voice said, "Mr. Dan Wink, please come to the courtesy counter."

My dad and I looked at Lance as he closed his cell phone and put it in his pocket. He smiled and waved at us. The rental car company had found us a car!

Our rental car was a ghetto mobile, as Lance called it. It was a bright shiny red car with really silver hub caps. The inside was a little torn up and the rear view mirror was held on to the ceiling with duct tape.

"This isn't so bad," my dad exclaimed, as we drove down Interstate 80, "as long as it gets us there!"

"It's a pimp mobile," my brother said, at the top of his voice!

I didn't know what a pimp mobile was and I wasn't sure I wanted to know.

I looked over at Chelsea who was texting feverishly. Chelsea's bag had been put on a flight to Cincinnati, Ohio so I'm sure she was texting all of her friends to let them know about her crisis.

"Ah, smell that air," my dad said.

"It smells like cow manure," my mom replied.

All of us kids giggled.

"It's the Midwest," my dad exclaimed! "This is where I grew up! Country roads, fantastic sunsets, air that smells like... well, manure."

We pulled into Columbus Junction, Iowa, the town where

Grandpa's visitation was to be held, around 6:00 p.m.

"Dad," I said, "how much further until we get to the hotel?"

"We should be at our hotel in about fifteen minutes," he answered.

"I can't wait," I said. "I have to use the bathroom. Could we please stop for a minute?" I said, pointing my finger at a grocery store on the right side of the road.

My brother and sister groaned as we pulled into the Econo Mart parking lot.

"I told you not to drink so much cola on the plane," my mom commented.

"I'll just be a minute," I said running into the store.

I found the bathroom and took care of business. As I walked out of the bathroom, I realized that my mouth tasted like a sewer, so I grabbed a pack of minty gum and headed for the checkout lane. I put the gum on the conveyer belt, and put a divider stick behind my gum so that the person behind me wouldn't get their groceries mixed up with my gum.

"Well, I am impressed!"

I looked around to see where the voice was coming from. It was the checkout girl.

"I am impressed," she repeated!

I looked over my shoulder to see who she was talking to, when suddenly I realized she was talking to me.

"I have been working all day," she continued, "and you're the first person, on my shift, in my line, to use the divider stick!"

"I didn't want my gum to get mixed up with the ladies Hamburger Helper behind me," I answered.

She kept talking while she sucked little bits of spittle through the side of her mouth.

"Why was I the lucky one to have this conversation?" I thought to myself.

"I HAVE BRAIN DAMAGE," she continued, pointing to her head, "AND EVEN I KNOW HOW TO USE THE DIVIDER STICK!"

I noticed that she had a small metal plate on the side of her head.

I got worried. She was talking so loudly. I leaned into her and tried to calm her down.

"I always use the divider stick," I agreed, "that way my groceries won't get mixed up with other peoples' groceries."

My eyes started to glaze over. I was tired from the flight and I hadn't gotten much sleep because I was upset about my grandpa. She continued to talk, ending each sentence with a question mark.

"That man in front of you? He had one item? He didn't use the divider stick? "

All of a sudden, a small piece of spittle flew out of the corner of her mouth. I watched in horror as it slowly flew through the air and landed on my left arm right above my wrist.

"The name's Ashlee Phipps," she said, extending her hand, "that'll be $1.05."

"Andy Wink," I said shaking her hand.

"Thank you for using the divider stick, Andy Wink!"

I paid for my gum and walked toward the car.

"Took you long enough," my brother exclaimed!

We got to our hotel at 6:30. Lance and I got to share a room and Chelsea would sleep on the sofa in the living room of my parent's suite.

"Holy crap," Lance shouted, as we walked into our room, "this room's like a room in a James Bond movie!"

Lance and I had a huge room with two giant beds and the bathroom was so big you could have landed a plane in it! It was huge! But the coolest thing about our room was the shower! It was a giant walk in shower and before you walked into it, you had to flip a switch on the wall so that a giant curtain would wrap around the shower for privacy.

"I'm taking a shower," my brother Lance said, "keep your eyes to yourself," he said as he closed the curtain.

I looked at a newspaper that was lying on the desk. A sticker on the front page said, "complimentary". I flipped through the pages of the paper and came across the obituary page. There was a picture of my grandpa.

I started to read.

———————————————

James Wink, 100, of Conesville, Iowa died Saturday, March 13 at the Columbus Junction Health Center. Funeral services for James will be at 9:00 a.m. on Wednesday, March 17 at the

Stacey-Lewis Funeral Home for Funeral and Cremation Services in Columbus Junction. Burial will be in the Indian Creek Cemetery. Following the services at the cemetery, a time of food and fellowship will be held at the Columbus Junction American Legion. Visitation for James will be held on Tuesday, March 16 from 6:00-8:00 p.m. at the Stacey-Lewis Funeral Home for Funeral and Cremation Services.

"6:00-8:00?" I thought to myself. "We're missing it!"

"Lance," I said, as I cracked the bathroom door, "we're missing it!"

"Get out of here you little pervert!" Lance shouted.

"Lance," I repeated, "the paper says that the visitation started at 6:00! We're already late!"

"Call Dad on my cell phone and tell him you little creep, and shut the door," Lance shouted!

I pulled Lance's cell phone out of his pants pocket and dialed my dad.

The phone rang and my dad picked up.

"What's up Lance?" my dad asked.

"It's Andy, Dad. The paper says that the visitation starts at 6:00!"

"Are you sure?" my dad asked.

"I've got the paper right here," I responded.

"Are you boys ready?" my dad asked.

"Lance is in the shower, and I have to put on my suit," I answered.

"We'll meet you in the lobby in fifteen minutes."

My dad hung up. I walked to the bathroom door and opened it.

"Lance," I shouted, "we're meeting in the lobby in fifteen minutes!"

"Get out of here!" Lance screamed throwing a bar of soap toward me.

I started to close the door when I noticed the shower curtain switch. I flipped the switch, laughing as the curtain slowly started to open. I quickly slammed the bathroom door shut.

"Andy!" my brother screamed.

By the time we got to the visitation, there were only fifteen minutes left.

My aunts, uncles, and cousins were all hugging each other. There were a lot of people there that I didn't know. Lance and I walked up to my grandpa's casket.

"That's not really him," Lance whispered, "I mean it is him, but it's just his body, his spirit's not there."

Lance started to cry.

"By the way, I'm going to get you for what you did to me in the shower!"

Lance walked away wiping his eyes.

"Why can't I cry?" I asked myself.

I kept looking at Grandpa. It looked like he was sleeping. He had on a navy blue suit and his arms were folded over his chest. I looked at the casket. It was bright and shiny, and all of the flowers that surrounded it were beautiful.

I continued to look at Grandpa, thinking of all of the great times I'd had with him, when I noticed a small open drawer that was part of the casket above my grandpa's chest. There was a golf ball in the drawer.

"I'm sorry about your grandpa," a man said as he walked up to me. "I'm Mr. Lewis, one of the owners of the funeral home."

"Hi," I said, shaking his hand, "I'm Andy Wink, this is my grandpa."

"He was my 5th grade teacher," he continued, "as a matter of fact, he taught a lot of people that were here tonight."

"What's the drawer for?" I asked.

"It's so people can leave a memory for your grandpa," he answered. After tomorrow's service, the drawer will be locked, and everything inside will be buried with him. See, someone's put a golf ball in the drawer. He played every day."

It was 8:00 and people were starting to leave. My dad and his brother, my uncle Tommy, decided to meet at the Cedar Crest golf course the next morning before my grandpa's funeral. They said it would be nice to hit a few balls in his memory. They said that Lance and I could come along, that it was kind of a "guy thing."

As I walked out the front door of the funeral home, I noticed Ashlee Phipps, the checkout girl from the Econo Mart standing by my grandpa's casket. I raised my hand and waved at her. She looked at me, squinted her eyes like a pirate, and slowly waved back. I wondered why she was there.

We headed out to the pimp mobile and went back to the hotel.

As I lay awake in bed I kept staring at the ceiling, and then I kept looking at the clock by my bed. 1:00 a.m. 2:00 a.m. 3:00 a.m. I couldn't sleep. Suddenly I sat up in bed.

"That's it!" I said loudly.

I decided I was going to write my grandpa a note and put it in the casket drawer.

I quietly got out of bed, so I wouldn't wake up Lance, grabbed some hotel paper and a pen, and went into the bath-room. I started to write.

Dear Grandpa,

I started to cry.

I feel kind of silly writing you this note to put in your casket, but what the heck....

I began to sob.

...I wanted you to know how much I loved both you and Grandma! I had so much fun when I was around the two of you and I'll always treasure the memories.

I don't know if there's a Heaven or not, but if there is, I know that you're there with Grandma and that you're both looking down at all of your family and friends that are celebrating your life.

I love you Grandpa and I'll miss you with all of my heart.

Your Grandson,
Andy

I couldn't stop crying. I put the note and pen on the floor next to me, crouched down, and covered my eyes with my hands. I stayed that way for a long time, crying and sobbing.

Suddenly the shower curtain slowly started to open.

"I told you I'd get you sucker," Lance exclaimed! "Hey what's wrong?" he said, as he walked into the bathroom.

"Nothing," I said, letting out another sob, "I'm sad."

Lance sat next to me on the floor.

"We're all sad," he said, "Grandpa was our last living grandparent, and we loved him."

Lance was right. Our grandma had died a couple of years earlier, and my grandparents on Mom's side of the family had died before I was born.

"It's sad," Lance said again, his eyes filling with tears. "You live your whole life doing these really cool things and then it all ends like this. It makes me hope that there's something better out there after it's all over."

I put my head on my brother's shoulder.

"I think that if you do good down here," he continued, "things will be okay. Live a good life, be happy, help others, have a family, things should be okay, and we'll eventually all end up together again somewhere, sometime."

"Do you remember when we were little how he took us fishing?" I asked.

"And do you remember the time you got the boat stuck on a sandbar when he let you drive the boat?" Lance answered.

I laughed, wiping my nose on my pajama sleeve.

"And do you remember how we always used to play baseball with Grandpa up by the old railroad tracks, and how he pretended that he couldn't hit the ball, when he really could?" I asked.

"And how we used to call him Boskie, after that Chicago Cubs player?" Lance answered.

"And how you broke the picture window when we played golf in the yard?"

"And how Grandpa used to pay us a dollar each to walk up the lane and pick up the mail?"

"Yeah, I remember," I answered, "and then we spent our money on candy at the Econo Mart?"

Lance and I sat there for over an hour sharing memories

of our grandpa. Finally he stood up yawning.

"You know what?" Lance asked.

"What?"

"I was really hoping you were sitting on the toilet when I opened that curtain!"

We both laughed as we got up and headed to our beds.

"Goodnight Lance," I said, as I turned off the light on my bed stand.

"Night Andy," Lance answered, as he rolled over on his side.

As I fell asleep I felt good. The crying had been good for me. I also felt good about Lance. I was proud that he was my brother, and I felt closer to him than I ever did before.

Dad woke us up at the crack of dawn, we put on our suits for the funeral, and then we drove to the golf course and met my uncle. He had a bucket of golf balls and some clubs with him.

"Let's head over to number seven," Uncle Tommy said, "that was your grandpa's favorite hole."

We walked to the tee off of number seven. It had a beautiful fairway and over to the right, by the rough, was a little pond. I looked toward the pond and saw Ashlee Phipps sitting on the bank.

"I'll be right back," I told my dad.

I walked toward the pond.

"What are you doing here?" I asked.

"I was thinking about your grandpa," she answered.

"You knew my grandpa?" I asked.

"Uh huh, we used to putt on the practice green over there," she said, pointing to a green to our left. "He paid me a dollar if I made it in one putt, fifty cents if I made it in two putts, and a quarter if I made it in three."

I smiled and sat down beside her.

"I heard your uncle talking last night about coming out here so I thought I'd join you. Your grandpa was a really nice man."

"Thanks," I answered.

"A really nice man," she repeated.

We sat quietly looking across the fairway. It was so green, and the sunshine lit up the dew on the grass like diamonds.

"This was your grandpa's favorite hole on the course," she said, lightly tapping the plate on her head.

"How did you hurt your head?" I asked.

"Car wreck," she answered, taking her hand away from her plate. "Sorry about your grandpa."

"Thanks," I answered.

"My grandpa died last year," she said.

"I'm sorry. I bet you miss him."

"I do," she said, "but I keep a part of him with me wherever I go."

She pulled a baggy out of her pocket that was filled with ashes.

"Yeah, yeah, I know I'm crazy," she continued, "I have a plate in my head, and I carry part of my grandpa's ashes with me, but you know what? It gets me through the day, being close to him I mean. Do you think that's weird?"

"No, no," I answered, "I don't think you're crazy, it's crazy, or weird."

I reached into my back pocket and pulled out the note I had written to my grandpa and handed it to her.

"I wrote my grandpa a note," I said handing it to her, "I'm going to put it in his casket today at the funeral. Do you think that's weird?"

She took the note and read it.

"That's really nice Andy," she said, handing the note back to me, "I don't think that's weird. I put the golf ball that we used to putt with in his casket last night at the visitation."

I folded the note and put it in my back pocket as we continued to look out across the fairway, each of us thinking quietly about my grandpa.

"Thanks for coming to my grandpa's visitation," I said, getting up, "and for coming out here and thinking of him. He would have liked that."

I started to walk away, stopped, and then turned to her.

"Are you coming to his funeral?"

"I have to work," she answered as she got up and put the ashes back in her pocket, "Andy?"

"Yeah?"

"The divider stick at the store? It's a metaphor for my relationship with people," she said.

She gave me a big hug and whispered in my ear, "Always remember, Andy."

She turned, and walked toward the club house. I headed back to my dad, uncle, and Lance who were hitting golf balls down the fairway.

"Who was that?" Lance asked.

"Someone who knew Grandpa," I answered.

We finished hitting the bucket of balls and then headed back to our cars.

"We need to hurry if we're going to get to the funeral on time," my dad exclaimed!

We got back to the hotel and it was 8:30. We had a half an hour to get to the funeral!

"Andy," my dad said quickly, "you go to the counter and check us out. The rooms have been put on a credit card, so just get a receipt. Lance, you go to your room and get yours and your brother's suitcases. I'll get your mom and sister. We'll meet back here in the lobby in five minutes!"

I walked up to the hotel counter.

"May I help you?" the woman at the checkout counter asked.

"I need to check out of our rooms," I answered.

"Aren't you a little young to be renting a room?" she laughed.

"I'm not that young," I answered.

"I'm just teasing you," she said, "what's the last name?"

"Wink," I answered.

She looked at her computer screen and said, "I hope you enjoyed your stay with us."

I thought for a moment.

"My brother and I liked the shower curtain," I answered laughing.

"Those are fun, aren't they," she answered. "Okay, your rooms are all paid for on a credit card, so you're all set."

She handed me the receipt, which I folded carefully and put in my back pocket.

I let out a sigh, met my family in the lobby, and headed to the funeral.

We got to the funeral home and walked in. My grandpa's casket was by the front door. I stopped, reached into my back pocket and put my note in the drawer next to Ashlee Phipps golf ball. I took one last look at my grandpa and went in and sat down. My brother and I were two of the casket bearers, so we sat with them.

As I sat there listening, I thought that my grandpa would have really liked this. Some of his friends and old students stood up and told funny stories about him, a lady got up and sang a really nice song, and the pastor gave a really great sermon talking about Grandpa and all of the things he had done in his life and the love that he had for my grandma and his family.

When the service was over, they closed my grandpa's casket and my brother and I, my uncle Tommy, and some of my cousins carried it out to the hearse. The casket bearers were told to ride in a limousine which would follow behind, which I thought was really cool because I'd never ridden in a limousine before!

The line of cars made its way down the winding country dirt roads of Iowa toward the Indian Creek Cemetery. I looked out the window at all of the flooded fields.

"We've had a lot of flooding this spring," Uncle Tommy said.

Suddenly, the tires of the limousine started to spin and we came to a sliding stop! I looked up ahead and the hearse had stopped as well, up to its back bumper in the mud. I turned and looked out the back window and saw the other cars turn around and go down another road.

"Stay here," my dad said, as he and Uncle Tommy got out of the limousine.

They met Mr. Lewis outside of the hearse and looked at the back bumper. Dad and Uncle Tommy came back to the limousine.

"Okay guys, everyone out," he said, "we're going to have to hoof it."

One of my cousins let out a small groan.

"It's okay Paul," my uncle said, "it's only about a mile."

"And all downhill," my dad added.

We got out of the limousine, slid the casket out of the hearse, grabbed a side of it, and started walking toward the cemetery. We were up to our ankles in mud!

"Dad would have loved this," my uncle laughed, as we continued walking.

We walked, and we slipped, and we walked, and we slipped. We slipped so much we were covered in mud up to our knees!

"Uh, Dad," I said, "I have to go."

"Not again," my brother said.

"I have to go too," said my cousin Paul.

"What do we do?" Uncle Tommy asked Dad.

"Let's set him down," my dad answered.

We carefully put the casket down on the muddy road and everyone went off to the side and took care of their business.

We came back to the casket, carefully picked it up, and finished our journey.

Everyone else had driven down different roads and met us at the cemetery.

The pastor started another sermon. When he finished, I felt my back pocket and let out a huge gasp.

"What's wrong?" my dad whispered.

"The hotel bill, I put it in the casket drawer with my note that I wrote to Grandpa," I whispered back.

I watched as the casket started to lower into the ground.

My dad started to laugh. He told everyone what I had done, and everyone started to laugh as well. They weren't laughing at me, they were laughing about where the hotel receipt had ended up.

"Well," my uncle Tommy said, "Dad always wanted to pick up the tab for everything and now he has!"

We laughed all of the way to the American Legion. Everyone had been under so much stress, it was exactly what we needed, to laugh, and Grandpa would have loved it!

We were so muddy, we had to hose off in back of the building and the water from the hose was so cold! Mom brought me and my brother each a pair of jeans, a Polo shirt, and another pair of shoes. She gave us each a big hug to warm us up.

After the food and fellowship at the American Legion, we said our goodbyes, and headed out of town so that we could catch our flight out of Chicago. We passed the Econo Mart and I thought of Ashlee Phipps. A big smile came across my face as I remembered what she had said, "Always remember."

As our plane took off from Midway, I looked out of the window at all of the houses on the ground and thought again to myself how small they were and how they looked like houses on a Monopoly board.

I pulled the journal Ms. Rife had given me for Christmas out of my coat pocket, opened it, and began to write.

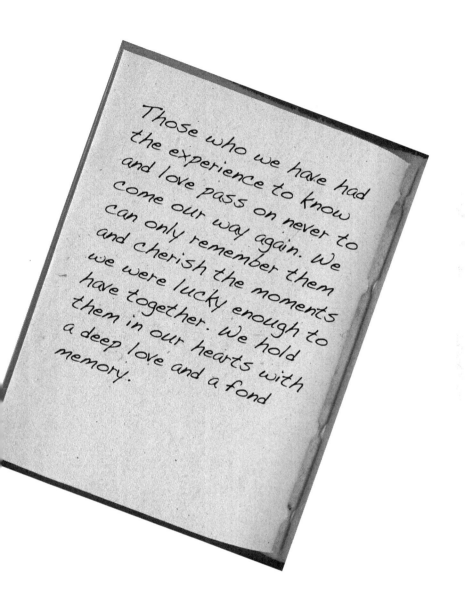

Those who we have had
the experience to know
and love pass on never to
come our way again. We
can only remember them
and cherish the moments
we were lucky enough to
have together. We hold
them in our hearts with
a deep love and a fond
memory.

Who knows what crazy
things will happen to us
in Hawaii!

Spring Break

7. It was Spring Break, and I Andy Wink was going to enjoy every minute of it!

I love Spring Break, not just because we get out of school for two weeks, but because of all of the craziness that happens to my family when we take a vacation.

Because of the craziness that's happened over the past two Spring Breaks, I've decided to give each part of this story its own title.

Spring Break- my dad

Let me start out by saying that my dad is one of the greatest men you'll ever meet! He's an attorney in Highlands Ranch, which is a suburb of Denver. Like me, my dad likes to help people which is why he's an attorney, I think, that, and probably because he makes a lot of money at his job. Dad is one of the wisest men I know and he always has a logical solution to the most difficult problems, unless they have something to do with him. Let me tell you a funny story about my dad and you'll understand what I mean.

Our Spring Break vacation to New York City was one of the best vacations ever! We went to the Empire State Building, we saw the Statue of Liberty, and we went to the Metropolitan Museum of Art and saw a lot of great art work. We went boating in the Central Park Boat Pond, we went to the zoo, we ate the biggest corned beef sandwiches and had the best cheesecake at the Carnegie Deli, and we saw the Broadway shows *The Lion King* (really great, amazing costumes and sets), *Mary Poppins* (kind of cool the way she flew over the audience at the end of the show, but the movie's better), and *Billy Elliot* (I liked the music and the dancing, but I didn't understand the politics or why the workers were striking.)

When our trip was over we were going to fly out of Newark, New Jersey. We were running late, we got stuck in traffic, and when we arrived at the airport we had just enough time to check our bags. We raced through the airport like the *Home Alone* family and when we finished going through security, Dad realized he had lost his car and house keys.

"I know I had them a minute ago," he said, "I tossed them into the security tub with my belt, shoes, wallet, and jacket."

The security guys helped Dad look in the tub, and they looked all over the floor around the metal detector. The keys were gone, and we had to go, otherwise we were going to miss our plane back to Denver.

When we returned to Denver, my uncle had to pick us up at the airport. (Our car was locked; the keys were gone.) And when we arrived at our house, Dad had to break in, which wasn't such a good idea because the burglar alarm went off, and the police came. (It took Dad about twenty minutes to convince the police that we lived there.)

After a few days, things started to settle down. We got the

house re-keyed, we picked up the car at the airport (with the spare set of car keys), and we all returned to our daily routines. All of us kids started school again, Mom took care of the house and carted all of us kids all over the place, and Dad went back to work to defend his clients in court.

One night, a couple of weeks later, Dad came home with a terrible pain in his foot.

"I was just standing there!" my dad said. "One minute I was feeling fine, standing in front of the Judge, and then all of a sudden, I felt a terrible stabbing in my right big toe!"

Mom thought this was unusual, so she took a closer look at my dad's right shoe. She reached up inside and pulled out Dad's car keys and house keys, the ones that he had lost at the airport in New Jersey. They had gotten wedged into his shoe when he tossed them into the security tub. Dad had worn those keys in his shoe from New Jersey to Denver, to work and back home again, and in Court. He didn't even realize that the keys were in his shoe, until they started to poke his right big toe.

Spring Break- my mom

My mom is what you call a stay-at-home mom, and she's the greatest mom in the whole world! She makes sure our clothes are washed, and she fixes my family these mouth watering dinners with the best desserts! She drives us kids to baseball, and hockey, and golf, and to our friends' houses, she takes my brother to work, **and** she volunteers at our schools!

With a husband, three kids, a dog, and a cat, my mom has her hands full! And let me tell you something, my mom can handle anything, and I've only seen her do one really crazy thing in my entire life!

This Spring Break Dad thought it would be fun to hook a camper to the back of the car and go to the Rockies Spring Training Camp in Scottsdale, Arizona. It was great seeing the Rockies play, and I got autographs from all of my favorite Rockies players; Todd Helton, Troy Tulowitzki, Jorge De La Rosa, Chris Iannetta, and Ian Stewart.

On the way home Dad thought it would be fun to go to a place called *Exotic Animal Park*. You know, it was one of those parks where you drive your car down these winding roads and you see all of these wild and exotic animals, kind of like *Jurassic Park*, except without the dinosaurs!

We saw giraffes, zebras, ostriches, camels, wildebeests, hyenas, llamas, and an elephant, and boy, let me tell you, did we ever see an elephant!

As we drove through the park there was an elephant standing in the middle of the road. Dad slowed the car down and honked the horn thinking the elephant would move, but it didn't. Dad stopped the car and honked the horn again, but the elephant still didn't move. After a few seconds, the elephant let out a loud trumpeting sound, his trunk sticking straight into the air, and then without any warning, the elephant sat on the hood of our car!

My mom and sister started to scream, my dad sat there in disbelief, my dog was barking like crazy, and my brother and I were laughing uncontrollably because all you could see out of the windshield was an elephant's butt!

All of the workers from *Exotic Animal Park* ran toward our car. They were screaming and yelling in Spanish, waving their arms, trying to get the elephant off the hood of our car, but the elephant didn't pay any attention to the workers. It was obvious to me that the elephant didn't understand Spanish, and why would it? Elephants are from Africa, not Mexico.

Suddenly the elephant started to get up, but then quickly sat down again, rocking the car up and down with its behind, the front bumper hitting the ground with each bounce!

"Hold on everyone," my dad shouted, grabbing the steering wheel!

My mom and sister screamed even louder, my dog stuck his snout out of the cracked window barking uncontrollably, and my brother and I kept laughing as loud as we could, holding our arms in the air like we were riding a roller coaster, and screaming out loud.

"Yeah, this is the best amusement ride ever!"

After a few seconds, the elephant stopped, got up, and slowly walked away. Even though we didn't understand what they were saying, the workers made sure we were okay, and amazingly, our car was too.

"I've had it!" Dad said.

He had been driving all night and the *Exotic Animal Park* experience had done him in. Dad was exhausted! He asked my mom to drive while he took a nap in the camper.

After a couple of hours of driving, Mom noticed that the car's tank was almost on empty. She pulled into a truck stop, filled the car up with gas, and headed back down the highway. What we didn't know, was that Dad, after drinking coffee all night to keep himself awake, had gotten out of the camper to use the bathroom. You guessed it. We pulled away from the gas station, thinking he was still asleep in the camper, and left my dad at the truck stop.

Dad had left his cell phone in the car, so there was no way of calling Mom. He couldn't remember her number, it was programmed into his phone, so he decided to go into the restaurant and have a piece of pie which is probably what most dads would have done if you think about it. Crisis and food. Dad figured that he was only a couple hundred miles from home. He would wait until we got there, call us at home, and then have my mom come back and pick him up. No big deal. Well, Dad is always great at starting up conversations, with everyone. He's just this laid back kind of guy and people trust him immediately. He told his story to practically everyone in the restaurant when one of the truckers said, "I'm going to go through Parker, I can give you a ride!" So Dad and the trucker hauled it down the interstate.

After an hour, Dad noticed that they were about to pass

our car. The trucker honked his horn and Dad hung out the window shouting and waving his hands.

"Hey, that looks like Dad!" I exclaimed.

"Don't be ridiculous Andy," my mom replied, "your dad's asleep in the camper!"

All of the honking and screaming must have scared my mom because she slowed down to a crawl, a turtle could have passed us.

"Thanks for the ride Cletus," my dad said after his trucker friend had dropped him off at our house. "My family should be here any minute."

"Take care buddy!" the trucker said as he pulled away waving.

Dad was about to take a nap on the front lawn when we came driving around the corner. Dad was shouting and waving as we pulled into the driveway. Mom was so shocked to see my dad standing in the front yard she drove the car and the camper right through the garage door. Boards and parts of the garage door and ceiling fell on top and all around the car. The front of the car went halfway into our laundry room. The elephant didn't dent the hood, but my mom did. It was the craziest thing I've ever seen my mom do.

This year for Spring Break we are going to Hawaii. Who knows what crazy things will happen to us there.

My New School

8. We were taking a field trip to our new middle school today and I, Andy Wink was excited! Our school guide, Mrs. Reedy, told us that when we went to Sierra Middle School, for lunch we could order hamburgers, tacos, salads, burritos, and Dominos Pizza! We also got to choose our classes we were going to take next year! I registered for Language Arts, Math, History, Life Science, PE, Art, Drama, and Technology!

We took a tour of the technology room. It was bigger and better than the technology room at our elementary school. They had state of the art computers! They also had video cameras that the kids could check out and film movies or commercials and then edit them on the computers! I would finally be able to film my own horror movie! I also decided that I was going to try out for the baseball team! I could tell as we took our tour that I was going to feel right at home!

As we walked through the hallways and classrooms, I got more and more excited! The hallways were bigger and we would each get our own locker! We would also get to dress out for PE!

All of a sudden, a lot of different thoughts hit me! I began to get apprehensive. There it was my big word for the day, apprehensive. It means to feel uneasy or fearful about something that might happen. I began to think of everything that could go wrong. What happened if I got lost? What happened if I didn't have enough time to get from one class to the next? What if I couldn't get the lock to my locker open? After PE, did I have to shower with the other kids? But most importantly, what if I didn't fit in?

Mrs. Reedy was amazing and she told it like it was! She said that middle school would be a time of great change for us. She said we needed to recognize the talents we were given, our strengths and our weaknesses, and that we shouldn't ever be afraid to try new things. She said we should join a club that would interest us, get involved in sports, drama, music, or maybe even an academic club, and by joining a club, it would be a great way to meet new friends.

She said middle school offered a lot of freedom, but sometimes, because of that freedom, we'd feel lost, because everything would move so fast. She said we'd have days where we'd feel like everything was falling apart and she said that when that day came, and it will, we should ask for help. If we didn't understand something, if we didn't know where to go, if we felt frustrated, we should ask or talk with someone.

She also said we should make a good impression. We should be always respectful to our teachers and the other students. She stressed that if we made a good impression it would make things easier. We were all in the same boat, and we needed to treat everyone the way we would want to be treated.

But the thing she stressed the most was that we are there to learn, so our grades are what mattered. Middle school was the beginning of a long journey and that journey would lead us down a road to what we would eventually become in life.

I took what Mrs. Reedy said very seriously. I loved the feeling of my new found freedom, but I also started to get a feeling of sadness and loss too.

I would miss my teachers at my elementary school. I'd miss the lunch ladies, I'd miss the friends I'd made, those who were moving away or transferring to another school, but most of all, I'd miss the security of being a kid. At middle school I'd become someone with responsibilities. Sure I'd still be a kid, but I'd have to start making a lot of my own decisions and make the right choices. I'd have to learn to manage my time and make sure that I had time for my homework and my after school activities. But most importantly, at my new school, I would become a young adult.

The bus ride back to our elementary school was hauntingly quiet. No one said much of anything.

"That was a lot to take in," Sean Bigler whispered.

"I thought it was awesome!" Palmer Pierson replied.

"There's so much to do."

"I'm a little scared," said Kevin Mackey.

"Of what?" I asked.

"Everything..." he answered.

I looked out the window of the bus at the melting snow and

the mountains in the far off distance. Spring was here but there was still a little chill in the air.

I looked at the people driving their cars down the road. One man was fiddling with his radio, a woman was talking on her cell phone, a little boy in the backseat of one of the cars was crying. I wondered where they were heading, and what they were going to do.

Life I thought. Everyone's got one, and it's up to each person to make something out of it. We learn something every day, life lessons, and like I've said before, through our life lessons we learn things, and become better people.

I was looking forward to my new school, to my seventh grade year, but I also wondered to myself, "What life lessons will I learn there?"

About the Author
Steve Paulding

Steve Paulding has been a teacher in the Douglas County School District since 1998. When he's not teaching, you can find Steve directing and acting in theatrical productions throughout the Denver area.

Steve grew up in Kirksville and Springfield, Missouri and he graduated from Truman State University in 1996.

Steve lives in Parker, Colorado where he continues to be inspired by his many students, family and friends.

About the Illustrator
Ben Spurgin

Ben Spurgin was born in Seattle, Washington on a beautiful November afternoon. His mother introduced him to classical music as an infant, and at age one, he showed a love of music, chanting "Mommy, la-la-la" as he stretched his arms toward the stereo. At age two he was asking, "Mommy, play the BIG music!." He began school in a "gifted" program for advanced students, and from age five & six was developing a love of electronics. He was always drawing little action figures on his school papers and he used Post-it note pads to create flip comics. At age seven he won a Young Author's contest sponsored by Seattle Pacific University, where his book is permanently archived in the children's section.

At age eight, Ben moved to Alaska. During summers with his mother, he learned the art of claymation (like Gumbi, and the famous California Raisins), placing a video camera on a tripod and a folded card table on the floor for his stage. He used Play-Doh and bendable characters for his frame-by-frame animation. He experimented with camera techniques & sound effects and began his life-long love of film making. Ben attended Diamond High School in Anchorage, where he and his best friend started their first garage band. At age 16 his mother bought him his first guitar which he mastered quickly. His genre of preference became heavy metal in all its variations. He was also a proud computer geek, and became a celebrity in the complex art of Flash animation, his favorite medium for creating a plethora of action hero films beginning with "Power of the Geek" and "Stick Slayer." Ben spent his adult years in Seattle exploring the bohemian side of life and developing a broad internet fan base for his music and films. His life-long goal was to spend seven minutes with Stephen Spielberg discussing his vision for the future of Flash integrated animation and film making.

Ben lived his last year in the Denver area where he was involved in theater, was a women's roller derby announcer, and of course, played in a band. He inspired many young artists and left a comet trail of creativity. He left us in mid-October, 2009 but his spirit continues to shine through tributes and memorials scattered throughout the internet, and through the stories exchanged almost daily by his family, friends and fans.

Made in the USA
Charleston, SC
15 December 2011